Dear Reader,

Life goes on, as anyone who's ever lost a loved one knows. The world keeps spinning, even if it spins out of control. The sun continues to rise and set, but sometimes our spirit has no ups and downs. Sometimes there's only numbness.

I believe in heaven...a heaven that is everything that life is not. Where colors are more vivid, and feelings are more poignant, a place where one's desires are instantly fulfilled, and one's dreams become reality. I believe in a heaven where people laugh, and play, and live forever.

But I also understand the anguish of those left behind.

That's why I wrote *Heaven Knows*. I wanted to explore a once-in-a-lifetime love, a heaven-on-earth, predestined kind of love, that was unexpectedly cut short by death. And I wanted to see it from both sides. From the one who was left, and the one who was taken.

I hope you'll be touched by Jason, my anguished angel who isn't ready for heaven just yet, and Sabrina, the wife he left behind, who's known only numbness for the three years since his death. And I hope you'll fall in love with the man Jason chooses to take his place.

Life. Round and round it goes. Where it stops...

Only Heaven knows.

—Tracy Hughes

ABOUT THE AUTHOR

Tracy Hughes began writing her first romance after graduating from Northeast Louisiana University in 1981. While in graduate school, she finished that book in lieu of her thesis, and decided to abandon her pursuit of a master's degree and follow her dream of becoming a writer. Her legions of fans are glad she did. Today, she is the award-winning author of over twenty-five novels, including series, mainstream and historical romance, as well as two novelizations and a screenplay. She has been honored with the industry's Golden Medallion (Rita) Award. Tracy was also a contributor to the bestselling and critically acclaimed "Calloway Corners" series, which was recently reissued by Harlequin. She lives in Mississippi with her husband and two children.

Books by Tracy Hughes

HARLEQUIN AMERICAN ROMANCE
381—HONORBOUND
410—SECOND CHANCES
438—FATHER KNOWS BEST
455—SAND MAN
502—DELTA DUST

HARLEQUIN SUPERROMANCE
304—ABOVE THE CLOUDS
342—JO: CALLOWAY CORNERS, BOOK 2
381—EMERALD WINDOWS
399—WHITE LIES AND ALIBIS

TRACY HUGHES

HEAVEN KNOWS

Harlequin Books

TORONTO • NEW YORK • LONDON
AMSTERDAM • PARIS • SYDNEY • HAMBURG
STOCKHOLM • ATHENS • TOKYO • MILAN
MADRID • WARSAW • BUDAPEST • AUCKLAND

This book is dedicated to Kelly Blackstock,
who knows heaven from the inside

ISBN 0-373-16542-0

HEAVEN KNOWS

Copyright © 1994 by Terri Herrington Blackstock

Printed in U.S.A.

Chapter One

Beneath Jason, the autumn trees exploded in a conflagration of yellows, reds, oranges and purples. In the photograph, Sabrina could only see his feet, for he'd somehow managed to take the picture from his hang glider.

He had been proud of that, and when he'd gotten it developed, he had rushed to her school where she'd been helping her students with their first abstract oil paintings, and had brandished the picture. "Wanna show your kids what heaven looks like?"

She wondered if it had lived up to the snapshot.

She turned the page of the photo album and saw Jason in his Duke University T-shirt with the hole in the shoulder, Jason standing waist-deep in a swimming pool with a tan she would have killed for, Jason with a charcoal Hitler moustache as he stood over the grill.

The photographs were beginning to fade, but the memories were as clear and crisp as they'd been the moments the pictures had been taken. By now, she should have put them all behind her and focused her eyes on her future. But nothing ahead of her looked quite as good as what she had left behind.

Sabrina closed the photo album and looked at the engagement ring gracing her finger. Anna had called it "a rock," and she supposed it was true. It was too extravagant for her. Within a year, it would be dulled with cookie dough, garden soil and sculpting clay. She had told Steven that she would have been much more comfortable with a smaller one, but he hadn't listened. He'd wanted to outdo what Jason had done for her.

She really shouldn't blame him.

Getting up, she went into the small room that she'd made into an art studio and office and got the stack of papers she had brought home from school to grade. She hadn't intended to grade them tonight, not with the engagement party tomorrow night and all the things she should be doing to prepare for it. But she was restless and needed a sense of normalcy. Her nails could wait, and so could her shoes. Preparing for the party would only remind her of Jason, as everything seemed to these days, and somehow she had to get her mind off him.

Turning off the light, she came out of the studio and from the corner of her eye caught a soft movement. "Is someone there?" she asked the quiet.

No one answered, and she went to the light switch, turned on the hall light and gazed up the hall. Still, she saw nothing.

Letting out a heavy breath, she told herself she had imagined it, and going back to the couch she sat down and began to scan the answers on her students' written test about Michelangelo.

But her mind wasn't focused, and again she felt as if someone was there watching her. Sitting up rigid, she looked around her. "Steven? If you're in here hiding somewhere, it isn't funny."

Or maybe it was Danny, trying to cheer her up with a little game playing. He had sensed her mood as the party approached, and he knew she was having a little trouble with the memories that had been assaulting her. "Danny?" she asked more tentatively. Still no answer. Getting up, she went to the closet and flung the door open. No one was there.

Sinking back onto the couch, she tried not to panic. If someone was in the house, wouldn't he have shown himself by now?

And then she heard it. Footsteps upstairs and a creak in the bedroom floor above the living room.

Trying not to panic, she grabbed a brass goose with a long beak that could serve as a sharp weapon, if she needed it, and tiptoed up the stairs.

The footsteps stopped, and she stood in the shadows, trembling, and threw on the light. Slowly she entered her bedroom and looked around. No one was there, and the closet door was open, leaving no hiding place. Nothing had changed.

Nothing except . . .

She took a step back and grabbed hold of the door as she saw the framed picture of herself and Jason lying on her bed. She hadn't left it there. She knew she hadn't. It had been on her dresser, next to the newer one of herself with Steven.

Who could have moved it?

She jumped as the floor behind her creaked, and she jerked around. But there was no one there.

She snatched up the phone to call 911, while she looked out her bedroom window into the night for evidence of a strange car or a prowler.

And that was when she saw it. The reflection of Jason in the window, as if he stood behind her, as if he were flesh and blood and had never died and left her alone.

Slowly she turned around.

Again, no one was there.

Tears rushed to her eyes, and her voice was hoarse as she whispered, "Jason?"

When there was no response, she told herself she'd imagined the whole ordeal and that she'd put the picture on her bed without realizing it and that she had only imagined Jason's face in the glass.

The tears came faster as she wilted onto the bed, realizing that her heart was still bruised even after three years, and that the yearning for him had only grown stronger, and that nothing—not Steven, not a new marriage, not even fulfilling her dreams of children—would ever make it go away.

"Oh, Jason," she whispered, picking up the framed picture and tracing a finger across his jawline. "I miss you so much."

Suddenly the chill she had felt before was gone, and she felt a sweet warmth circling her. It was as if Jason really was there, responding to her pain, comforting her, loving her as he always had.

She wanted to bury herself in that warmth, cling to the memories of her husband before the accident and fend off tomorrow. But that was impossible, she told herself finally. Tomorrow always came, with or without Jason. That was the hellish part about being left behind. And only heaven knew how much longer she'd have to feel this way.

THE GLASSES CLINKED as the guests—many who had traveled to North Carolina for the occasion, even though they planned to come back a month from now for the wedding—all drank to Steven's father's toast, something about a lifetime of happiness, prosperity, and sundry other things.

"Aren't you going to drink, darling?" Steven asked.

Sabrina looked at her champagne. "Uh...my stomach's a little upset, Steven."

"Do you want me to find the head caterer and have her track down something for you to take?"

She smiled. "No, I'm fine. Honestly."

She looked at Steven as another of the guests made another toast to them, and she recalled why she'd been so attracted to him. The first time she'd seen him, when she'd been at his stockbrokerage firm investing some of the money Jason had left her in mutual funds, she had been stricken with those eyes. They were a strange mixture of blue and green, and had caught her attention immediately. She hadn't known then that his eyes were really brown, and that the color came from contact lenses. She supposed that didn't matter.

But she remembered looking at him and seeing him watch her with a grin in those eyes. He'd seemed playful, almost like Jason, and she'd felt the chemistry between them instantly when he'd asked her to lunch.

He was the first date she'd had since Jason's death, but everyone had said it was time. It had been almost three years. She had to get on with things. So she had tried.

She'd never expected to be standing at her engagement party only twelve weeks later, planning a wedding that wasn't even a month away.

He drank to his uncle's toast, and Sabrina smiled and tried to look cordial. His black hair was perfectly in place, and she wondered if he spent more time on it than she spent on hers. Then, ashamed of herself, she told herself that she hadn't had enough sleep last night, and she was getting a little crazy.

Thankfully, the toasting stopped, and the music started up. Stepping down from the dais, she tried to plaster on that serene smile she knew she should be wearing, but it wasn't easy. The tears were stalking again, and Sabrina knew that if she didn't get out of the party right away, she would break down in front of all of them and embarrass Steven. This was supposed to be fun, she told herself. A prelude to the wedding that was just around the corner. A prelude to the life she would share with Steven. But still the tears stalked.

Pushing through her future gossips-in-law, she headed for the French doors. A few of the black sheep from either her family or Steven's—she honestly couldn't remember which one—called out to her over the music, but she pretended not to hear. Averting her face so they wouldn't see the incipient tears in her eyes, she opened the double glass doors to the veranda and slipped out into the night.

The fresh air enveloped her, as the silence did, and she wished from her heart she could keep walking until she could find her car where the valets had parked it, get in it and drive away without looking back.

But she should be ashamed for even entertaining such a thought at her own engagement party. Jason would have said she needed an attitude adjustment. And she did, she told herself. It was time to stop looking back and clinging to those futile memories. It was time she started looking ahead of her, to her life with Steven, to the children they would have together and the dreams they had already begun planting.

But as she counted off the promises her future held, she wondered desperately why the feeling just wasn't there. All she felt tonight was the smothering sensation that things were moving too fast, that she was sinking and was unable to save herself.

But that wasn't fair to Steven. It wasn't his fault she kept comparing him to Jason, or this wedding to her first.

Her hand trembled as she wiped her tears, and she stood straighter and took a deep breath to calm her before she went inside. A chilling breeze swept through the weeping willow at the center of the hotel ballroom's courtyard, making the leaves shuffle and whisper in quiet conspiracy.

"He doesn't make you laugh like I did."

Sabrina swung around and saw a man standing in the shadows, and a shiver of awareness coursed through her as she struggled to see his face. "What?" she whispered.

"I said, he doesn't make you laugh like I did, Bree, and you know it."

Those tears assaulted her again as her heart responded to that deep, confident voice, that voice she only heard in her dreams these days. Stunned, she gaped at the man in the darkness, knowing but not believing that he stood there, as casually as if he had every right to waltz back into life, as if he made his own choice whether to exist or not.

Slowly she took a step closer until his face became clearer. "Jason?" she whispered on a breath of astonishment.

"Yeah, babe, it's me."

It was Jason, as virile and big and charismatic as she remembered, but... It couldn't be him. Too much wine, she told herself. Too many whirling emotions. Too many memories. Closing her eyes, she turned and started back to the hotel, but he grabbed her arm and swung her around.

"Whoa, there, babe. Don't be scared."

She gaped at his hand still grasping her arm, and through her sleeve she felt his warmth and the reality of his grip. Catching her breath on a sob, she whispered, "Jason? It can't be you. I know it can't."

"Here I am," Jason said. "Look at me, Bree."

Her eyes were luminous as she turned her face to him, adoring the sight of his just-shaven face, his broad shoulders, his towering height. She could feel the heat of his presence, smell the scent of Tide and Pert shampoo, hear him breathing. "Am I going crazy, Jase, or are you standing here, flesh and blood?"

The smile that was so common to his eyes faded like a candle blown out by the wind. "Maybe we're both going a little crazy, babe. Maybe that's why they let me come. But I'm not really flesh and blood."

Brace yourself, she told herself. *It's just a dream...like so many others.* But wasn't it time for those dreams to fade? Wasn't it time for another man to dominate them for a change?

But there was something about this one that seemed too real for a dream, something about the way he gazed at her, as if he, too, had been hungry for just one more look, as if he, too, welcomed madness if it meant being face-to-face with her again.

"You're not a ghost, Jason. I don't believe in ghosts. Besides, I can feel you, and you smell the way you always did."

His smile returned to his emerald eyes, and he chuckled. "Not a ghost, I don't think. Maybe more like an angel. Or something in between. They never really label us like that. Doesn't matter, I guess."

"No," she whispered, wiping her tears. "It doesn't matter." A sob stole her breath away, and her mouth trembled as she reached up to touch his face with tentative fingers. He closed his eyes as she slid her hands into his hair. For a moment, he looked as if he might stop her, but as the torment grew greater on his face, he bent slightly to meet her, as he had done a thousand times before. Slowly, his arms slid around her.

It was a crushing homecoming, and as he held her, her body was racked with sobs. She felt him shaking with emotion, as well, felt the warmth that she hadn't been able to experience since his death, felt all the empty, dead places inside her stirring to life.

But after a moment, and much too soon, he pushed her away from him. His eyes were misty as he looked at her. "We're not supposed to do this. They were very specific about that."

"Who?"

"You know. My committee. The heavyweights. They told me not to touch you."

Her brown eyes caught the moonlight as she gazed at him. "Then why are you here?"

His eyes grew softer, more urgent. "I had something to tell you, babe, so I got special permission. You wouldn't believe the bureaucracy. Dozens of committee meetings, inquiries, investigations, emotional evaluations—"

She shook her head. "What are you talking about?"

"Heaven," he said. He let her go and raked both hands through his brown hair, leaving it tousled. "It's a terrific place, but I seem to be messing it all up. See, you're supposed to be happy there, only I wasn't exactly, so they started making all these concessions. Anyway, that's not the point."

She laughed through her tears, loving the way he'd always digressed and the way he somehow miraculously found his way back to his punch line.

"The bottom line, Bree, is that this wedding is a big mistake. I convinced them to let me stop you."

For a moment she only stared at him, and as his words began to sink in, she took a step back. "What do you mean, stop me?"

"The guy's a jerk, babe. He doesn't deserve you. You need to lose him."

"No." She took another step back, shaking her head. "I should have known this would happen. I've read books. New attachments always bring these . . . these memories or . . ."

"Hallucinations?" he provided patiently.

"Whatever," she said. "Part of me is still clinging to you, and this is my brain's way of telling me that I have to let you go." She sucked in a shaky breath and wiped her tears again. "Besides," she went on, "you were always the jealous type. You could never stand the thought of me with another man."

"Jealous?" he repeated incredulously. "Hey, I'm not jealous. You want to tie the knot with some crooked stockbroker who can't wait to get his hands on the money I left you, then go ahead. No skin off my teeth."

"He is not after my money!" she returned. "He's a wonderful, decent man."

Jason gave a mirthless laugh. "Yeah, right." He looked at her again, his anger putting up a barrier between them, but she had dealt with it before. It never lasted very long. "Besides, you're getting your story screwed up, Bree. Either I'm a hallucination or I'm a jealous husband. Which is it?''

The question threw her off guard, and she clutched her head. "I—I don't know."

He set his hands on his hips. "Okay, then, I am a little jealous, but I wouldn't be with just any guy. He's the *wrong* guy, Bree."

Suddenly she was exhausted, and she wondered if she'd have the energy to get through the rest of the evening. This was crazy. All of it was crazy.

"It's true, what I said, you know. He doesn't make you laugh."

Her sigh seemed to take the last ounce of energy from her. "I haven't laughed in a long time, Jason."

He touched her face in that sweet, gentle way he used to, and wiped her tears with the callused pad of his thumb. "I know that, baby," he whispered. "And it eats at me. But there's somebody down here who *can* make you laugh. This Steven bozo just isn't the guy."

Again that inexplicable anger filled her, and she found herself struggling with the logic of it. It was just like after his death, when she had alternated between agony and rage. And she had prayed, over and over again, that time could be turned back, that his accident could be erased. She had thrown bargains up to heaven, promising a life of perfection if only he could be brought back to her. But then, when those prayers went unanswered, she had turned her rage to Jason for having the gall, the unmitigated insensitivity, to leave her without saying goodbye. Even now he wasn't here to give her closure, but to divert her from a course that she was determined would make her happy. And she found that the rage was still just as fresh as the agony.

"I'm getting married, Jason. I'm moving on. And if it's the last thing I do, I'm going to let go of you! Because I've been alone for the last three years, and I'm tired of being alone!"

Before she knew it, he was holding her again, and she rested her head against his chest, felt his heart beating against her face. It was as if he was real and could take her home and hold her all night and permanently dry her tears. There was nothing else that felt as sweet as his embrace, nothing more comforting. Melting in that comfort, she wept against his chest.

Then suddenly, as if he'd never been there at all, he was gone.

Coldness swept over her, and she stumbled back, searching the shadows from which he had emerged. "Jason!" she cried.

But there was no answer. A whirlwind of emotions—frustration, despair, confusion, anger—swirled around her heart, constricting it with fist-like strength, making her want to strike out at the world for playing such cruel games with her.

She heard the door to the hotel open, and the sound of music and mingling overflowed into her silence. "Sabrina?"

Tearing her eyes from the shadows where she'd first seen Jason, she saw Steven coming toward her. Dread washed over her, and her soul pleaded with her to leave this place now and find some sanctuary in her quiet home. But she had obligations here, and she wasn't one to shirk her commitments. Not even if Jason told her to.

Wiping her eyes, she tried to smile. His eyes virtually glowed, as if he'd never had more fun, and she told herself not to ruin it. He didn't deserve to be brought down tonight.

Sweeping her into his arms and twirling her around, he said, "Isn't this a fantastic party?"

"It's great," she said, though her voice betrayed her lack of enthusiasm.

He stopped dancing and stepped back, frowning at her. "Honey, are you okay?"

"I'm fine," she said, trying to laugh off her tears as she reached up to sweep a stray black hair from his forehead. But there was no laughter in her heart. "I just got a little overcome with emotion. All these people here, celebrating with us . . ."

The tears rushed her again, so she turned her back to him. Steven slipped up behind her and put his arms around her. He wasn't as big as Jason, and his embrace didn't feel quite as strong or warm. *There I go again*, she thought, *comparing the two*. It wasn't fair, because Jason was gone and Steven was here. *That* was the bottom line.

"They're happy for us," he was saying, "because everybody knows it's going to be a perfect union."

"Everybody?" Hopelessly, her eyes searched the shadows.

"Well, if there's anybody who doesn't, they haven't told me."

For a moment she was quiet, but finally that survival voice inside her told her to get a grip. She was just confused. She was just tired. Her mind was playing tricks on her, and her heart was so weary.

"You're right, Steven," she said, taking a deep breath. "It is the perfect union." Steeling herself, she took his hand and began to lead him to the door. "Our guests will wonder where we are. Let's go in."

"Wait a minute."

Tugging on her arm, he drew her to him, and his fingertips were gentle as they caressed her jawline, then lingered on her neck. "They can wonder a few more minutes while I take advantage of this beautiful night with my bride-to-be."

Gently, he kissed her, and she felt herself opening to him, though she wasn't sure if it was out of need or desire.

It was she who finally broke the kiss, and stepping away from him, she hugged her own arms. "I'm cold, Steven. Let's go inside."

If he noticed a chill in her mood, he didn't show it. He only put his arm around her to keep her warm, and led her into the party.

THE REST of the engagement party that should have been a landmark occasion in her life crept by, as friends and relatives and acquaintances of Steven congratulated her with silly anecdotes about her fiancé, whisked her around the dance floor and forced her to feign a good time. There were few of her own friends there, and as she scanned the crowd for them, she realized that she had isolated herself for the last three years. Clinging to only those friends who remembered Jason and the way they had been as a couple, she had effectively blocked out new friendships, as if they would mean leaving her husband behind. Until Steven.

A man tickled her waist, and she turned and smiled at Danny, Jason's childhood friend and the man who had become her closest friend. The sight of him made her smile instantly.

It was hard not to, for he always wore a mischievous grin in his blue eyes, and the way he wore his sandy hair these days—too long for a lawyer but befitting a bachelor on the prowl—always made her want to finger-brush it into place. "Danny, I was afraid you'd left by now. Anna left half an hour ago."

Danny shook his head dolefully, but that amused glint in his eyes remained. "No, I'm afraid I had too much hope of finding Ms. Right in this crowd. You've got to hand it to Steven. He has good-looking cousins."

"That's what attracted me to him right away," she deadpanned. "This family has great genes. If you overlook the insanity."

Danny threw his head back and laughed, and Sabrina was instantly ashamed. "I didn't mean that."

"Yes, you did," Danny said.

Trying to change the subject, she asked, "So did you have any luck? With finding Ms. Right?"

"Not really." He feigned disappointment. "Unless you count Lucille, who has hair growing out of the mole on her nose. She liked me."

"Moles can be removed."

"Not this one. It goes way down into her personality."

Sabrina shoved playfully at his chest, but her amusement stopped just short of laughter. It was only then that Danny's grin faded, and a slight frown drew his brows together. "You haven't been crying, have you, kiddo?"

She sighed and glanced awkwardly around. "Is it obvious?"

"Just to me," he said. "But then we both know I'm psychic."

It was a standing joke based on the silly character he played at parties, wrapping a towel on his head and pretending to read people's minds. But it didn't seem funny tonight. And for a moment, she struggled with the urge to tell him she had seen Jason, touched him, talked to him. He had been Jason's college roommate, his law partner, his best friend. He had loved Jason like a brother, and had grieved almost as hard as she over his sudden death. Wouldn't he believe her?

But then another part of her warned her to keep quiet, or Danny might think that Steven wasn't the only one with insanity genes in his family.

"I don't know what's wrong with me," she said, blotting at her eyes. "I can't seem to stop these tears."

"Hey, don't worry about it. It's your party, and you can cry if you want to."

She breathed a laugh. "Danny?" she asked, glancing out over the dance floor where Steven two-stepped with one of his aunts. "What do you think of Steven?"

"Seems like a decent guy, from what I've seen." He looked at the sobriety on her face. "Hey, what's wrong?"

"I don't know." Shaking her head as if to clear it, she said, "I should be having the time of my life. But I keep thinking about—"

"You've got to stop that, Sabrina," Danny cut in. "Jason wouldn't want you dwelling on him, always looking back. You need something to look forward to."

"Well, if a wedding won't do it, I don't know what will."

Concern softened the smile in Danny's eyes, and he tilted her face up to his. "Hey, now. What's going on in that head of yours?"

Tears came to her eyes, and she tried not to look so distraught. "Oh, Danny. I went outside a little while ago and—" No, she thought, stopping herself. It was too crazy, too much to expect anyone to believe. Tempering her words, she said, "I felt Jason's presence. It was like he was standing in front of me."

Danny issued a long sigh. "Darlin', I feel him, too, all the time. There's nothing wrong with that."

"This was different."

He didn't scoff at her or test her for fever or tell her to get over it. As always, Danny listened, as if getting news he hungered for about a dear friend. "Different how?"

Evading the question, she got right to the point. "I don't think he approves of Steven."

Danny laughed. "Yeah, well, that would be no surprise. Jason always did go ballistic when another man looked at you."

She caught Steven's eye across the dance floor, waved at him and fixed her smile again. "Yeah, I know."

"Hey, Sabrina," Danny said, and she glanced at him. "Steven's no Jason. But there was only one Jason." He studied her for a moment, his eyes seeing too much of what she hid inside. "Hey, are you okay with this marriage thing? Because there's no hurry if you're not."

"Yeah, sure, I'm great," she said less enthusiastically than she wanted. "I'm just a little tired."

"I could take you home, if you want. I'm leaving now myself."

Tempted, she glanced at her fiancé. "No," she said finally. "I'd better stay for the duration." She wiped the mist gathering at the corners of her eyes. "Sorry about this," she whispered.

He grinned and kissed her forehead, and a sweet warmth burst through her. "It's time for you to cry happy tears, darlin'. If that's not what these are, maybe you should put the brakes on."

She nodded, wishing he wasn't always so perceptive. "I'm okay, Danny. I'll call you tomorrow."

She watched, feeling suddenly alone, as Danny slipped out the side door and left her at the mercy of the crowd.

LATER THAT NIGHT, as the last of the guests was leaving, Sabrina gravitated to the courtyard, where Jason had confronted her hours before. If he had truly been there, she thought, maybe he would come back. Their time had been too short, and it was cruel to give her just a moment to revive her memories and open the not-yet-healed wounds in her heart, only to snatch him away again. But she had lost her faith in fairness a long time ago.

Stealing away, she walked behind the weeping willow to the garden blooming just beyond. He could be there now, watching her quietly, making judgments on her decisions.... Or he could be longing for her as she longed for him, wishing for one more moment of absolute love before he turned his back on her forever.

But it was just another empty hope, she thought, for there was no one there. Her eyes filled with tears, and she looked up at the moonlight, trying to imagine a heaven where Jason stomped around in a tizzy, complaining about being jerked away from life too early, frustrated about what she was doing with her life and using his attorney skills to persuade the powers that be to let him come back to tell her so.

The thought struck her as funny, and through her tears she began to laugh. "Oh, Jason, you fool. What am I going to do with you?"

He didn't answer, but she felt as though he was there, listening to every word and brooding over the fact that she hadn't called off the wedding yet.

Her amusement faded, and she stood in the dark quiet, feeling for the man she had loved more than life itself, listening for the man who had taken her joy with him when he'd left her.

"Out here again?"

She swung around, as if she had been caught cheating, and saw Steven coming across the courtyard. His eyes still sparkled from the fun he'd had at the party, and she realized that he thrived on these events. Especially when they were in his honor. "Yeah. It's a beautiful night."

He grinned and leaned down to kiss her. "You're a beautiful woman. And next month, you're going to be my beautiful wife."

She tried to smile. "I have a lot to do. Just moving is going to be such an ordeal. I've lived in that house forever."

"If I didn't know better, I'd think you were dreading it."

"No, that's not it at all." Her protest was a little too strained. "It's just . . . it's hard to let go of all those memories."

"We'll make our own memories, honey. It'll be terrific. You'll see."

"I know." Sighing, she tried to sound exuberant. "And those memories start with tonight, huh? That was some party."

"Yeah, and it looks like I made some great contacts, too. My cousin Cheryl's husband wants to meet tomorrow to talk about starting his portfolio, and my aunt Jackie wants me to invest the life insurance money she got when my uncle died. Do you know what kind of commission I'll get off that?"

"No, Steven."

"A lot. Trust me, it could be my biggest account yet."

"Is that why you enjoyed the party so much? Because you were making all those terrific contacts?"

He recognized the bite in her voice, and his smile faded. "Of course not, Sabrina. I enjoyed it because it was ours."

She looked at her feet, knowing she was picking a fight and not entirely sure why. "I'm sorry, Steven. I'm just really tired. I guess I'm a little cranky, too."

His arms came around her again, and she laid her head against his shoulder. But as she did, she couldn't help comparing his build to Jason's. There was a good four inches difference in the two men's height, and there was something about the protective way Jason held her that made her feel so secure. . . .

But Jason was dead, and Steven wasn't. Why did she keep having to remind herself of that?

"Well, let's get you home so you can rest. My mother plans to call you early tomorrow to go shopping for your dress."

She pulled back. "Steven, I didn't agree to that. I haven't even decided what kind of dress I want, or what color."

"Honey, time's running out. You have to find something. Besides, I want you to wear white. We're having a traditional wedding, and it's only right."

"It's not my first wedding, Steven," she said. "We've been all through this."

"Well, it's *my* first. I want my bride in white."

She sighed. "I just—I want it to be different this time. I still have special memories, Steven. I don't want to replace them."

"So you're determined to downscale this so that it can't possibly compete with yours and Jason's wedding?"

Was that what she was doing? she asked herself as she stared at him. "No," she said. "It isn't a question of competing. It's a question of wanting it to be something new and fresh, something different, so it doesn't remind me of the first time."

"Everything about it reminds you of the first time," he said. He took her arms, forced her to look up at him. "Sweetheart, it's you and me now. It's time to forget Jason. He's not coming back."

"I know that!" Her face reddened, and not sure why that fact seemed so cruel to her, she jerked her arms free. "But can't you respect the fact that I want this wedding to be different from my first?"

"I can respect it if you wear white!"

She glared at him. "Steven, you're being unreasonable."

"Tell it to my mother," he said. "She doesn't have daughters, and I'm her first son to get married. She has visions of a beautiful wedding, and a beautiful dress."

"Then *you* wear the dress!"

She couldn't believe she had said that, and as they stared at each other, she felt ridiculous. It was just a dress, after all. Just a stupid white dress.

"I'm sorry," she said suddenly. "Really. I didn't mean that."

His smile was the slightest bit condescending. "I didn't think you did. Now, when my mother calls—"

"I'll be ready," she said, lifting her chin. "And we'll shop together."

"And you'll seriously look for a dress? With an open mind?"

"Of course."

"Good." He leaned down and kissed her again, but any tenderness was lost on her. All she wanted was to go home and be alone, where she could recall seeing Jason again, replay it in her mind and feel warm with it just for a little while.

THE FLOWERS that arrived bright and early the next morning reminded her why she was marrying Steven. Like the morning sun raiding her living room, they brightened her outlook and made Jason's appearance the night before seem like a silly dream.

She shopped with Steven's mother that morning, cordially trying on everything she suggested and telling herself that she could wear white if it meant that much to them. It wasn't that big a deal, after all.

By the time they got home, Elaine, her future mother-in-law, had bought herself two dresses, both of which were too tight for her but which she swore would fit by the wedding, since she vowed her diet would drop twenty pounds from her hips. Sabrina had allowed her to buy two white dresses for her, neither of which she was crazy about but which she could choose between when her head felt a little clearer.

Danny was pulling into her driveway when she got home, and the sight of a friendly face filled her with relief. Getting out of the car, she said, "Am I glad to see you."

"Why? What's going on?"

"I've been shopping with Steven's mother. I think it may take a couple of days to recover."

She unlocked the door to her Victorian home and pushed inside, Danny on her heels. "I found two dresses," she said, tossing her keys on the table. She flung herself into Jason's favorite recliner and pulled the footrest up. "They're making me wear white."

"Who's making you?" Danny sat down in the other recliner and pulled his feet up. As if he lived there, he reached for the remote control and flicked on the television.

"Steven. It's not that big a deal, really."

"You sure? It's your wedding."

She didn't answer for a moment as he flicked from channel to channel, never stopping to view anything for more than two seconds. "Danny? What do you think Jason would think of Steven?"

"That's the same question you asked me last night." Danny stopped flicking and gazed at her.

"I'm starting to think it has more significance than you're telling me."

"It does," she admitted. "Really. Aside from the jealousy factor, what do you think Jason would say?"

Danny sighed. "I don't know if he'd like him, Sabrina. He's not the type he would have chosen for a friend. You know, he's a little too upper crust."

"Upper crust?"

"You know. The family. The upbringing."

She gazed for a moment at her friend. "Oh, you mean he's a snob. Is that it, Danny?"

Danny looked uncomfortable and went back to flipping. "No, that's not what I mean."

She got up and went to stand in front of him. "Danny, look me in the eye and tell me the truth. Do *you* like Steven?"

Again the flipping stopped. "Come on, Sabrina. It doesn't matter what I think."

"I need to know, Danny. Tell me."

Danny looked at her. "You take things too seriously, you know that? Lighten up."

"Do you or don't you like him?"

"He's okay, what I know of him."

"I should have known." She jerked the remote control out of his hand and set her hands on her hips. "You're just like him."

"Just like who?"

"Jason, that's who! You're in cahoots, aren't you?"

Danny laughed. "You're crazy."

"Don't I know it." Frustrated, she tossed the remote control back to him and turned to the picture of Jason on her mantel. "You know, I should have put this away by now. Steven will insist on it. I'll have to get rid of all the pictures."

Danny's voice was quiet when he finally answered her. "You could give them to me. I'd get a kick out of having them."

Her eyes were a little too shiny when she turned to him. "Really? You want them?"

"Well, yeah. I didn't have that many."

She picked up the framed photograph and feathered her fingers across the glass. "I don't know," she whispered. "It's gonna be hard giving them up."

"Yeah." Danny looked at the remote control, flicked off the television and set the control down. "Hey, remember that time we all went to that water park?"

She smiled. "Yeah. Who were you with? Linda What's Her Name?"

"No. Brenda What's Her Name. And you and Jason raced us down the slide and cut us off so that we all wound up falling off our mats...."

"And tumbling down in a jumble of arms and legs..."

"Which was the closest I ever got to Linda."

"I thought you said Brenda."

They both crumpled in laughter, and as it faded away, Sabrina sighed. "Gosh, that felt good. I haven't laughed in a long time."

"Steven doesn't make you laugh."

She shook her head. "That's what Jason said."

"Jason?"

She caught herself and quickly started toward the kitchen. "I mean, he would have said that. Come on. Let's see what's in the fridge. Then I have to get ready for my date."

Danny pulled up and followed after her. "Did I tell you about *my* hot date tonight? The cutest little redhead. I met her at the gym this morning. She liked my pecs."

"Yeah, and I bet you liked hers."

He grinned. "Sure, but it was her mind that most attracted me to her."

"Right," she said, opening the refrigerator door. "And at the end of the date, the two of you will probably sit around and discuss acid rain and peace in the Middle East."

He grinned. "Well, no. But if we did, she could hold up her end."

"My point exactly," she said, laughing.

Danny reached for an apple on the bottom shelf, bit into it and considered her for a moment. "Hey, Sabrina, are you sure about Steven? You seem to have an awful lot of doubts lately."

She sighed and closed the door without taking anything. "Cold feet. That's all it is. It's normal, isn't it?"

He shrugged. "I guess. But I don't remember you feeling this way when you married Jason."

"I didn't, Danny." She slid onto the counter and pulled her feet up. Hugging her knees, she looked at her friend. "But I'm not sure you can feel that way twice. It just doesn't happen."

"So you have to settle for feeling less?"

She groaned and dropped her face against her knees. "I'm not settling, Danny. I love Steven. He's everything I've been waiting for. When I'm with him, I hardly think of Jason at all."

"Wow. That's quite an endorsement."

She shot him a dirty look. "It's more than that, and you know it. I can be happy with him. He's a good man." She glanced at the flowers she'd set in a vase that morning. "See? He sent me those flowers today."

"Um. Flowers." He nodded. "They're nice."

She didn't miss his lack of enthusiasm, and it almost made her angry. "What is it, Danny? Spit it out."

He took another bite, thinking about what he wanted to say, and finally went for it. "It's just that…ever since I saw you crying last night at your engagement party, I've been feeling like maybe you're making a mistake. I don't know, Sabrina. It's just a hunch, but I'm worried about you."

"It's prewedding jitters, for heaven's sake. I'm fine."

"Just be sure, okay, darlin'? This is for life."

"Yeah, well, life can be real short."

For a moment he only looked at her, then finally tossed the apple into the wastebasket. "If you're married to the wrong person, darlin', it can be longer than you ever imagined."

"Or if you're alone."

He smiled. "You're never alone, Sabrina. You know that." He messed up her hair, then pointed to her nose in that silly way he had and started out of the room. "Gotta go now."

She waited until he had made it through the foyer and she heard the front door opening before she said, "Danny? Stop worrying about me, okay?"

"If you say so," he called back. "Phone me tomorrow."

"You call me."

"Yeah, yeah. Check you later."

She smiled as she heard the door close behind him and told herself that it was time she got over this madness. First she had her dead husband bringing up a barrage of doubts, and now Danny, who never had a care in the world. And she knew where it all originated. Somewhere deep in the back of her mind. It was fear of abandonment. Fear of another death. Another grieving period. Fear of being left alone again.

But Steven wouldn't die. God didn't take two husbands in a row, did he? No, she told herself. This would be the man she'd grow old with. Steven would be the one to romance her in the nursing home.

The thought seemed neither comforting nor realistic, but she clung to it nonetheless. For it seemed infinitely more sane to her than believing her dead husband was going to guide her to the right person.

Jason would rather have served a term in hell than see her with another man. Look how far he'd gone already to keep her from marrying Steven. Coming back from the dead, for heaven's sake! She'd known his jealousy knew no bounds, but she'd never expected it to go this far.

Something about the thought suddenly struck her as funny, and she began to chuckle and shake her head. Not even heaven could change Jason.

But she sure wouldn't be surprised if Jason was able to change heaven.

Chapter Two

Jason rapped three times on the door, waited for it to open and stepped over the threshold into the bright room to which he'd been summoned so many times. They were all there waiting at the table, Peter with that white crew cut that made him look like a negligent Hari Krishna, Dave with a slingshot in his hip pocket and a loose-leaf notebook full of his latest poetry, Mo, in a pair of baggy Bermuda shorts and a net shirt, sipping on a glass of lemonade with an umbrella sticking out.

Jason supposed he should count his blessings that these were the ones on the committee. All of them were kind souls, if a little eccentric, and they understood flexibility. If he'd had to deal with someone a little more legalistic, someone like, say, Elijah, there might be no reasoning with them.

"Come in, Jason."

Jason approached the table and reached out to shake their hands. "Hey, Pete. How's it goin'?"

"Not bad, for heaven." Peter winked at the other committee members, and everyone laughed. "Sit down, Jason," he said, still chuckling.

Jason took his seat, thankful that they were all in good moods. But the truth was, they were always in good moods. It was hard to be in a bad mood in heaven. Personally, he'd had to work real hard at it.

"So, now that you've had the opportunity to speak to your wife, Jason, we just wanted to touch base with you and see if you're feeling freer now to enjoy what we have for you here."

"She didn't listen. I have to go back."

Peter groaned and gave meaningful looks to the others at the table. "Come on, Jason. We've been more than patient with you. We can't let you go back. It's just not done. We made an exception for you once, but that's all."

"But she's going to ruin her life, man," Jason said, leaning forward at the table, his eyes intent on convincing him. "This guy's bad news. I want her to be happy, Pete. She's not over me yet—I mean, who could blame her, but—"

Dave harrumphed. "Who, indeed?"

"I'm talking grief, man. It's been three years. She should be on her way to finding happiness by now."

"Tell us about it," Mo exclaimed. "That's what we've been saying about you."

"It'll make me happy to see her happy," Jason said. "Come on, guys. Let me go back one more time. She's gonna marry this guy, and I'm telling you, it's not in the plan...."

"She's free to divert from the plan, Jason," Mo said.

Jason shot him a disgusted look. "Yeah, yeah, I know all about that free-will clause, Mr. Forty-Years-in-the-Desert, but sue me for wanting to save her a lifetime of misery." Instantly, he realized he'd made a mistake. It wasn't wise to insult the ones who would be making this decision. "Look, I'm sorry," he said quickly. "I'm just a little..."

"Cranky?" Peter provided.

"Well, yeah. You can't blame me."

"It's heaven, Jason!" Dave declared. "When are you going to get that through your head? Nobody is cranky in heaven!"

Jason sighed. "Look, I know I'm driving you people crazy. Just bear with me. I'll be happy as soon as I know she is. But right now... She's not thinking clearly, guys. She's lonely. She thinks he can make her feel good again."

"Speaking of making her feel good again..." Peter put on his John Lennon glasses and studied the file in front of him. "It's come to my attention, Jason, that you didn't follow our orders when you saw her. We told you in no uncertain terms that you were not to touch her. In fact, that's why you were called back sooner than we planned. You broke the rules."

"Aw, man. I knew you were gonna get to that." He leaned back in his chair, rubbing his temples, not because he had a headache—he hadn't gotten one since he'd been here—but because old habits died hard. "You just don't understand. She was so...so beautiful." His voice cracked and dropped to a softer timbre. "And she was crying. What could I do? Stand there and watch? I had to hold her just for a minute."

"And do you think that made her feel better? Did it make *you* feel better?"

Jason thought for a moment, and suddenly he found his eyes misting over in a way he never would have allowed them to on earth. Especially not in front of a bunch of men. "I felt better for about thirty seconds," he whispered. "Until I had to let her go." He sighed and tried to focus on the ceiling. "It felt so good to hold her again."

"We set those rules for your own protection, Jason. We don't want to see you so unhappy."

"Then let me go back. Let me help her get on the right track. Let me point her to the right guy, and then, I swear, I'll leave her alone and be the happiest camper you've ever seen."

"Good grief." Sighing, Peter took off his glasses and leaned back in his chair. "And what if you break the rule again? What if you touch her, or kiss her, or heaven knows what else?"

"I messed up, Pete. Sue me. It's not like you've never made a mistake. I seem to recall three very famous ones you made once."

Peter looked hurt, and Dave intervened. "That was a long time ago, Jason."

"Yeah?" Jason asked. "And what about you with Bathsheba? I don't recall you keeping your hands to yourself when you met her. You thought I forgot that, didn't you?"

Dave glared at him. "See, that's the thing I hate so much about celebrity. Nobody ever forgets the negatives, but if you do something good, do they remember that? No."

"You see, Jason," Mo threw in, "we're not without our own past mistakes. That's why we understand you. That's why we set rules. We know how destructive mistakes can be. Hey, I never got to see the Promised Land. You think that didn't tear me up? But the truth is, heaven isn't supposed to be a place of punishment." He looked at the others and sipped on his lemonade again. "What do you say, guys? If he vows not to touch her again, and knows the consequences if he does, couldn't we let him go back? Just one more time?"

Jason held his breath as Peter nodded, then waited for Dave, who still sulked. Finally, Dave sighed. "All right, Jason. One more time. But if you break the rules, it's ix-nay. You won't ever be allowed to appear to her again."

"Aw, thanks, guys," Jason said, jumping up. "This is great. Really great."

They laughed at Jason's sudden jubilance—surprised that such a small thing could make him happy when none of heaven's grandeur could—and finally Peter waved his arm. "Go on. Get outa here."

"LOOK AT ALL THIS JUNK. We'll never fit it all in the new house." Steven opened the flap of a box full of old books that had been stored for years in Sabrina's attic, and shook his head. "You'd make a fortune if you had a garage sale."

"I was going to donate some of it to charity," she said.

"Good idea. I'll call the Salvation Army to come haul it all off, if you want."

"No." She closed the box as if he had disturbed some spirit's quiet slumber. "I want to go through everything first. Some of it's important."

"Anything unimportant enough to be stored in the attic should be thrown away, honey. We need to start our new life fresh, unencumbered."

"We will," she said. "I promise."

He smiled at her with that what-will-I-do-with-you smile and swept her into his arms. "Just think. In two weeks, we'll be on a plane to Vienna."

That comfort she had felt when she'd first met him washed over her, and she smiled at him. "Vienna. It's hard to imagine, isn't it?"

"Not really. Mr. and Mrs. Steven Bishop will be doing a lot of traveling."

She slid her arms around his neck and tried to picture it. "Are we going to be happy, Steven?"

"Forever," he promised.

"And are you going to grow comfortable and start taking me for granted?"

"Probably."

Playfully, she slapped at him, and he laughed. "Never. I'll never take you for granted."

Her grin faded and she looked seriously at him. "Will we laugh, Steven, and dance, and smooch in front of the television?"

"All of the above."

She tried to cling to his promises, knowing that a future with him meant happiness and fulfillment, but some voice in the back of her mind told her it wouldn't be exactly that way, for it wasn't that way now.

Steven kissed her, long and wet, and she longed for the shiver of awareness and anticipation she used to get with Jason. Shouldn't she react more physically to Steven? she asked herself. No, that was impossible—lately she'd been heaping so much pressure on herself to think and feel things she didn't think or feel. It would never be the same as it had been with Jason. But it could be different. And maybe, as the years went by, it could even grow into something better.

Steven wiped a smudge off of her cheek, then started to the stairs. "I have to go. I have some paperwork to catch up on."

"On Sunday?"

"Yes, on Sunday. I'll never get rich keeping eight to five hours, you know."

"Is that what you want, Steven? To get rich?"

"Isn't that what everybody wants?"

She shrugged. "Not me."

"That's easy for you to say. Jason left you well provided for."

"Jason's life insurance didn't begin to make up for what I lost."

"I know, darling," he said. "I'm just saying that it's easy for people with money to pretend money doesn't matter. But it does matter. You'd realize that if you lost it."

"I don't live off it, Steven. It's been in the bank earning interest since he died."

"You should spend it," he said. "Live a little. I'll help you."

An uneasy feeling rose in her heart, and she tried to smile. "I'm not going to spend it, Steven."

"Fine," he said without batting an eye. "Then we'll invest it someplace where it earns more money. I've been thinking about it and—"

"You've been thinking about what you're going to do with my money?"

He looked at her. "Come on, Sabrina. Do you trust me or don't you? That's what I do for a living. You're good at creative things, and I'm good at financial ones."

She wanted to fling back that she didn't need anyone managing her money, but part of her knew that wouldn't be fair. When she married him, everything that was hers would be his, and vice versa. As he'd said before when they'd discussed finances, it would all go into the same pot.

Had that been his idea, or hers?

"Gotta go now." He kissed her again, then started down the stairs.

"I'm going to stay up here and sort some of this out," she said. "You can let yourself out."

"All right," he said. "By the way, if you hear someone out in the front yard, it's probably Anna putting the for-sale sign up. I told her to bring you a listing agreement this morning."

"So soon?" Her heart sank, but she tried not to show it.

"We've been all through this, honey. The sooner we sell your house, the better off we'll be. The money would be much better invested somewhere else."

"I know, but . . . it's just all happening so fast."

"Not fast enough," he said. "See you later."

Sabrina waited until she heard the front door close downstairs, and slowly she slid down the wall until her bottom hit the floor. Hugging her knees, she looked around at the remnants of her past that she didn't want to part with.

Jason had always called her a pack rat, but he had kept as many sentimental things as she had. She opened the flap of the box of books and pulled out the first paperback she touched. It was *The Hobbit*, by J.R.R. Tolkien, and she leaned her head against the wall and remembered how they had both loved the book about those little people in that fantasy world, and the fact that it was one of the first things they'd discovered they had in common. She had kept a picture of Gandalf she had painted in her studio over her table. Most people thought it was Merlin, or some cultish figure they couldn't name. But the first time Jason had walked in he had taken one look and whispered, "Gandalf."

It was magic, the kind the wizard himself had been able to concoct, and the coincidences and common interests had made it even more so.

They had both known every word to Dan Fogelberg's "Be On Your Way," and they both got tears in their eyes singing it. They each had every Leo Kotke album that had ever been released, though none of their other friends had ever heard of the guitar master. They both had those late-for-a-test dreams, a weakness for pistachios and a love of Chinese food.

They had both loved deep, wet, long kisses, gazing into each other's eyes and whispering "I love you" in church.

And they had both believed in happily ever after.

They had been wrong about that.

She turned to another box, flipped open the lid and saw the collection of rocks she and Jason had gathered the time they'd gone to the Roanoake River for a third—or was it fourth—honeymoon. They had ridden the rapids for three days, until they were too sore to even walk, and then they had driven across the state to the Blue Ridge Mountains, where they had taken hang-gliding lessons for a week. It had been the closest she'd ever gotten to heaven, and not because she had navigated the sky with nothing but a piece of canvas above her. It was because she had been with Jason.

But even in Durham, where they'd made their home, she had felt pretty close to heaven. It wasn't until Jason was gone that that feeling had slipped away. The colors on the trees hadn't turned such vivid shades of red and yellow and purple since he died, and the sky hadn't seemed as blue, and winter seemed much more barren and cruel.

Closing the box, she went to the rack she had in the corner, where she had hung all of Jason's clothes in zippered bags. They waited there, as if he would return one day and wear them again, but now she supposed it was time to give them away.

She unzipped one of the bags and pulled out the shirts that hung there. She had bought them all for him, or they had bought them together, for Jason had always hated shopping for himself. If it hadn't been for her, he would have worn threadbare shirts or nothing at all. Preferably the latter.

Taking one of the shirts from the hanger, she wadded it and brought it to her face and breathed in the scent that still reminded her of him. Then, shaking it out, she pulled it on, hugged herself in it and pulled the collar up to her face to breathe in more of its scent.

He was there in every fiber of it, his scent and his warmth, and she felt him as if he had taken it off only seconds ago.

"It looks better on you than it did on me."

Sabrina's heart jolted, and she swung around, knocking down a stepladder and almost losing her balance. Jason stood there, amused, as real as he'd ever been. "You're making me crazy, Jason. I'm gonna have a heart attack."

"I know, babe. Sorry about that."

For a moment she stood there, staring at him, and finally she launched forward to throw her arms around him, but he held out his hands and backed away. "No, don't touch me. If you do, they won't let me come back."

As if she'd hit some invisible wall, she stopped cold and dropped her hands to her sides. "I won't touch you."

For a long, poignant moment they stared at each other, so sweet, so familiar, so longing....

For lack of purpose, her arms came around herself. "You look...so beautiful," she whispered.

"Me?" He shook his head, admiring her with sweet intensity. "You . . . you still take my breath away."

Their eyes locked and held again, and finally he realized he wasn't going to accomplish a thing if he kept looking at her like this. Tearing his eyes away, he looked around the attic. "Lot of memories here, huh?"

"Yeah." She went to the box of books and pulled out *The Hobbit*. "I was just remembering . . ."

"Gandalf."

"The magic." She smiled and straightened the collar of the shirt she wore. "And I was trying to decide what to do with your clothes. Any ideas?"

He walked across the floor, his footsteps vibrating on the planks that he had laid himself, always intending to make the attic into a nursery when they had children. But they had never gotten that far.

He looked through the clothes in the bag she had unzipped, grinning as he remembered each piece, and finally he turned to her. "Funny that you'd want my opinion about who should get my clothes but not who should get my wife."

Sighing, she whispered, "Jason, a lot of time has passed."

"Yeah, but you still sleep in my T-shirts at night and sit around in the attic wearing my clothes and remembering the magic."

"But that's no kind of life." Her voice broke, and tears came to her eyes.

"I know that," he said. "And if I knew that you could be with the right person and be happy, then I'd leave you alone and get busy enjoying eternity."

"Steven is the right person."

"No, he's not, Bree. He's got ulterior motives. He's up to no good."

"What are you talking about? What kind of ulterior motives?"

"You're worth a lot of money, Bree. The house itself is worth a fortune, and the life insurance money—"

"Stop it!" Her voice wobbled as she faced him with fire in her eyes. "You're not going to convince me that a man can't love me without trying to get something out of it."

"No, Bree. *I* know what a treasure you are. But some people are so dumb that they can pass up wonderful treasures in their pursuit of dollar signs."

"Steven's not like that."

"Fine. Then test him. Get a prenuptial agreement. Refuse to sell the house. Tell him you've decided to give your money to charity. He'll not only have what my grandmother used to call a hissy fit, he might find a reason not to go through with the wedding."

"Well, of course, he would, Jason! It would indicate that I'm crazy."

"If he really loved you, it wouldn't matter. It never bothered me."

Ignoring his attempt at humor, she curled her hands into fists. "Oh, you make me so furious. You're asking me to pick a fight. Cause trouble on purpose. Why would I want to do that two weeks before my wedding?"

"You have to test him, Bree. You can't just marry him after knowing him three months and assume that things are the way they appear."

She turned her back to him, her face burning, and finally she swung to face him. "It's the sex thing, isn't it? You can't stand the fact that I'll have sex with him."

"Well, the fact that you haven't already says a lot for your level of passion. I know we had trouble keeping our hands off each other before we were married. I haven't noticed you taking a lot of cold showers."

"You're not always here. You don't know if I do or not."

He laughed then, raising her anger to a nuclear level. "I'm here enough, Bree. I know what's going on. As pure as your morals are, your sex drive is too strong for a simple kiss good-night without another thought. I think you're not as attracted to him as you say."

"You are so full of it," she said. "You don't have any idea how attracted to him I am! How do you know that's not why we pushed the wedding up?"

His chuckle was maddening. "I know he pushed the wedding up because your CD expires next month. He plans to get it out of the bank you have it in and put it in some high-risk stock, in his own name."

The matter-of-fact way he threw out that information was like ice water being casually thrown in her face. "That's ludicrous. He chose that date because it's my birthday. He loves me, Jason, and he wanted me to be his wife when I turn thirty."

"Test him, Bree. Please test him."

Her face reddened. "You're not supposed to test the people you love! What kind of marriage will we have without trust?"

"Exactly. And what kind of marriage will you have if your trust is being broken?" He took a step toward her, his eyes beseeching her to listen. "Bree, do you honestly think I'd go to all the trouble of coming back here to lie to you?"

She shook her head and backed away. "No. You're just grasping. You don't want me to marry anyone, so you'll do anything to keep me alone."

"How could I lie? I live in heaven, for Pete's sake! You think they'd let me come down here to lie to you?"

"You're not even real!" she shouted. "You're just a figment of my imagination."

"Well, if that's the truth, then you need therapy, baby, not a new marriage."

She collapsed against the wall, giving in to her tears. "Damn you."

"Too late."

For a moment, he watched her cry, helpless to comfort her, and finally his own tears welled in his eyes. Stepping toward her, he reached out as if to stroke her hair, but his hand didn't make contact. "Don't cry, baby."

She tried to catch her breath on a sob. "Don't you understand, Jason, that if I had a choice, I'd always choose you? No one else even comes close. But I don't have a choice. You're gone!"

He dropped his head and wished he could dispute that, but he couldn't.

"And now you're coming here, making up things about the first man I've even been remotely interested in in three years, messing me all up...."

"I'm not making it up, Bree. And it's not just jealousy. There is a guy who's right for you. He's fun and has a great personality, and he cares about you a lot, and he's as alive as they come, which I guess is a big plus these days. And I approve of him."

"Who?" she asked, doubt dripping from her voice.

"I'm not supposed to tell you. They hate it when people spill the beans. You're supposed to do a lot of contemplating and praying and stuff, and then make up your own mind. But hey, I'm not real confident that you'd make the right choice."

"Who, Jason?" she asked more forcefully.

"Who loves you?" he asked. "Who would have stolen you away from me if he hadn't loved me almost as much?"

She frowned and waited.

"Who can make you laugh? Who seems familiar? Who understands?"

It came to her in a flash, like the answer to a prayer, but it felt strange to utter it. "Danny?"

"Bingo!"

She shook her head. "You'd hate that. He's your best friend."

"Who better to take care of my baby?"

"But...we're too good friends. We've never thought of each other that way."

"Correction. I happen to know he's thought of you that way. He has a picture of you in his bedroom."

"No."

"But there's a little guilt involved on his side, too. He feels like he might be betraying me somehow if he makes a move. Not that I can read minds, you understand. I can't. I'm just telling you what I've observed."

She started to shake her head and held out a hand to quell him. "No. That's not possible. Danny's my pal. I love him like a brother."

"You can feel differently about him, Bree. You just have to change your thinking. Try it. It'll feel a heck of a lot better than you feel with ol' Steve."

"I love Steven."

"No, you don't."

She wanted to hit him, but she didn't dare touch him, or he might never be able to come back. "Sometimes, I would just kill you if you weren't already dead. You make me so angry."

"Maybe. But it's only because you know I'm right."

"You're not right."

"Then test it, Bree. Ask for a prenuptial agreement and see how he tap-dances his way out of it. Give him the idea that you'll never let him touch your CD. He'll give himself away."

"Jason, you're asking me to trick the man I'm marrying in two weeks."

"Don't do it, Bree. Please, don't do it. Have I ever asked you for anything before?"

She wiped her eyes. "Only to fall as deeply in love as it's possible to fall, then to let you go without any warning."

"Okay, that was a biggie, but it wasn't my idea. I mean lately."

"No," she said with a weepy laugh. "You haven't asked for anything lately."

"I'm asking you now to just check out what I've told you. Just because I'm the only man you've ever really loved, and I happen to have an omniscient insight into these things, doesn't mean you should trust me."

"You're so darn cocky," she said.

"But I'm cute."

She grinned and tried not to giggle, but she failed. "Yes, you are."

Their laughter faded into whispers and breaths until their smiles were gone and their eyes were full. "I wish I could hold you again," he said.

She sucked in a sob. "Wouldn't it be great?"

"If it's any consolation, Bree, I've grieved for you, too. Even in heaven, and they keep telling me that it's just not done. They're at their wits' end."

"It isn't any consolation," she whispered. "I'd like to think one of us could be happy."

"Both of us can," he said. "Fall in love with Danny. Laugh a hundred times a day. Have ten babies, and let all of them look like you. Name one after me. Then I'll be happy."

The emotion in her throat made it difficult to speak, but after a moment, she said, "I love you, Jason."

"Oh, baby, I love you, too."

Her eyes fluttered closed, and she felt her heart stirring as it always had when he told her he loved her, coming to life and reminding her how dormant it had been, showing her a light when she hadn't known she was in darkness.

But when she opened her eyes, he was gone.

Settling back into the darkness, she hugged his shirt more tightly around her, buried her face in the collar and tried to hold on to that feeling of unencumbered love for as long as it lingered.

Chapter Three

The thought of tricking Steven into some kind of apocalyptic anger seemed absurd to Sabrina. She wasn't the underhanded type. Yet she had to know if any part of what Jason had told her was true. But how? Should she spy on him? Should she wear a wig, sunglasses and a trench coat, and spirit all over the place behind him, waiting for him to do something wrong? It was ridiculous. Just ridiculous.

But it was also necessary that she do at least some of what Jason had suggested. If, indeed, he really wasn't just a figment of her yearning imagination, then he knew things she didn't know. Jason would never lie to her. Not even in her dreams.

She heard a car in the driveway and looked out the window. She saw Anna Riley, her closest girlfriend and the one she'd chosen to be her matron of honor, parking and going around to the back to open the trunk.

She was the realtor Steven had signed to sell her house, but the thought that Anna had taken him at his word and not contacted Sabrina about the timing rankled her. But it was silly, she thought. What else would she do with the house after she got married? She certainly couldn't live here. It wasn't nearly opulent enough for Steven, and besides, he wanted her to start clean, fresh, without all her memories of Jason. She couldn't say she blamed him. She would expect the same thing from any man she married.

She just didn't know why it was so hard to give.

The doorbell rang, and sighing, she went to answer it. Anna greeted her with an overwide smile on her face and a For Sale sign in her hand. "Ready to make a lot of money?" she asked.

Sabrina's stomach tightened. "Anna, didn't it occur to you that Steven doesn't own this house? You can't list it unless *I* tell you to."

"Well, I know that. I just thought— Well..." Her shoulders drooped, and she shoved her long blond hair out of her face. "Sabrina, are you mad at me?"

"No," she said, letting out a heavy breath and abandoning the door. She heard it close behind Anna as she came in behind her. "I'm just having trouble letting go of the house."

"All right," Anna said, catching up to her and taking her by the shoulders. She guided her into the kitchen and sat her down at the table. "Sit down here, and I'm gonna make you a cup of coffee, and we're going to talk. What's wrong?"

"I don't know," Sabrina said. "Cold feet, maybe. I've been trying to clean out some things, and the memories kind of got hold of me."

"It's Jason, isn't it?"

She looked at Anna and nodded. "Yeah. It's hard letting go, Anna. This house meant so much to us."

Anna filled the coffeemaker, quietly contemplating Sabrina's words. "I remember when you moved in," she said. "You had a couch and a bed. That was all."

Sabrina smiled. "I thought we'd never get it all furnished." She looked at the ceiling, her eyes shining with memory. "Remember all those auctions?"

Anna laughed softly. "How many Saturday afternoons did I go with you? Sometimes we'd come home with nothing...sometimes something wonderful."

"That's the thing," she said. "There's so much of Jason in every piece." She looked around, and her eyes fell on the antique sewing machine table in the corner of the kitchen. "Remember when I wanted that piece, but Jason told me it was too expensive?"

Anna smiled. "And then he made a deal to buy it from the highest bidder, and had it delivered on your birthday. That was the first time I had ever seen you cry."

Sabrina sighed. "Sure wasn't the last."

Anna poured the coffee and brought a cup to Sabrina. Sitting down, she said, "I'm sorry I didn't consult you about the house. I've just been delirious that you were so happy, that you were starting over. And I thought we could save you the trouble if I just let Steven take care of it."

"I know," she said. "And you were probably right. Go ahead and put the sign up."

"Are you sure?"

"Yeah." But her voice didn't sound sure. "If anyone's going to make a commission off of it, I want it to be you."

"It's not about commission," Anna said. "I just can't wait to see you settling down into a happy life with a future. Even if it means leaving the old one behind."

"Why doesn't that sound good to me?" Sabrina whispered.

Anna gazed at her for a long moment. "Maybe you're not ready, Sabrina."

"The wedding's in two weeks."

"There's no rush."

"That's easy for you to say when you're already married." Sabrina pulled her feet to her chair and brought the cup to her lips. She closed her eyes as the steam coated her face like a gentle spirit's caress. "I've got to get a grip."

"Why don't you stop gripping and just relax for a little while?"

"You're right," she said. "I know you are." She smiled at her friend and made a conscious effort to relax. "Thanks, Anna. You can put the sign up now. I can deal with it."

"You know, you don't have to go through with selling it. You can change your mind anytime you want."

"I know. And it's not the house, so much."

"No, Sabrina, it's not. But it's time for you to be happy. I'm rooting for you, you know."

She smiled. "I've got a lot of people rooting for me." She finished the coffee, then set the cup down hard. "Tell you what. Just lean the sign against the house, and when I'm ready, I'll put it on the lawn, okay?"

"Whatever you say. Now, are you ready to hear the plans for your shower? I've already sent all the invitations. Steven's mother brought me a list with about two hundred names on it. If they all show up, we might have to have it out in the yard. My house may not be big enough."

"The yard's fine," Sabrina said, sinking back into her chair. "We'll all bring blankets and sit on the grass."

"Right," Anna said, starting to laugh. "We'd have to have ambulances standing by, though, because Elaine and her friends would have a collective coronary."

"This isn't Elaine's wedding," Sabrina said. "It's mine."

Anna didn't buy her sudden toughness. "Right. And you're the person with two dresses in your closet, neither of which you wanted in the first place."

"So, I'm a wimp."

"No." Anna sighed. "If you were a wimp, I'd have a sign up on your lawn instead of leaning against your house. And Steven wouldn't have any reason to blow his top when he comes by this afternoon."

THE SIGN LEANING on Sabrina's porch was like a hostile intruder waiting for her to drop her guard, and she wished she'd never agreed to leaving it there. Resentment grew inside her like a misplanted weed, and she knew that if she didn't get rid of it now, it was likely to snuff out all the good feelings she had about the wedding.

And she did have good feelings. Lots of them. Steven was just what she needed—a good and honest man who would love and cherish her and give her a wonderful family and a lifetime of happiness. If she could just stop clinging to her past, she knew she could feel good again.

She went into the dining room, the only room that didn't have an area rug covering the hardwood floor that Danny and Jason had polyurethaned before they had moved in. She kept the floor here bare for a reason.

Slowly, she sat on the cold, smooth floor and felt for the small deviation in the finish. There it was, she thought, angling her head to see the faint outline of a footprint.

Jason's footprint.

She smiled at the memory of how angry he'd been at himself for running across the just-polyurethaned floor to answer the phone. Danny had laughed until his ribs hurt, even though it meant sanding the floor all over again. They had never been able to remove the prints completely, but there had been many times over the last three years she had been glad for them.

It was the only house in the world with Jason's footprints, and the thought of selling it almost made her ill.

Outside she heard a car in the driveway, and she knew it was probably Steven. She tried to smile when she opened the door to greet him.

"Why isn't the sign up?" he asked as he came up the walk carrying his briefcase.

Her smile was defensive, and she sighed. "I wasn't ready."

"Ready?" he asked. He went into the kitchen, dropped his briefcase on the table and got a cup out of the cabinet. "What do you mean, ready?"

"I mean, it's a big step." The coffee Anna had made was still in the pot, and as he poured a cup, she went on. "I wanted to talk to you about it."

"So talk," he said. "What's on your mind?"

She took a deep breath, clinging to Jason's words. *Test him, Bree.*

"I'm thinking about hanging on to the house for a little longer." Bracing herself, she turned her face away.

"You can't do that. We can't afford it."

"Can't afford it?" Breathing a dry laugh, she looked at him. "It's paid for, Steven."

"No, I mean it's silly to hold on to a vacant house that you don't need. If we sold it, we could buy a big new house, and free up that money."

"We're going to have plenty, Steven. Besides, I was thinking of keeping my studio here. I'm inspired here."

"You're a teacher, Sabrina," he said with marked chagrin. "What do you need a studio for?"

"I'm an art teacher," she said. "I need a place to work on things when I'm not at school."

"When you're not at school, I'll want you home," he said.

His argument made her uneasy, and finally she faced him squarely. "What is it, Jason? Why does this bother you so? It's my house."

For a moment he struggled with his answer, but finally, seeming defeated, he slumped back in his chair. "It bothers me because I think it's your way of hanging on to Jason. Sabrina, you can't blame me for wanting us to start with a clean slate."

"I don't have a clean slate, Steven. That's too much to ask."

"Is it too much to ask for you to love me whole-heartedly, without constantly comparing me to your first husband?"

"No, of course not."

"Is it too much to ask for you to stop dwelling on your memories of your time with him?"

"No."

"Then I want you to sell the house. If you love me, you'll do what I ask."

She poured herself a cup, and hugging the warmth of it, sat down and pulled her feet onto her chair. "Why does that feel like an ultimatum?"

"Because you're distorting things. You're nervous. And maybe, deep down, you're afraid to commit yourself to someone a hundred percent again, for fear that you'll be hurt again."

She thought about that for a moment, wondering if there was any truth to it. Honestly, she wasn't sure.

He reached across the table and took her hand, feathered her fingers open with his fingertips and pressed a kiss on her palm. "I'm not going to hurt you, Sabrina. I promise. And I'm not going to leave you or disappoint you or die on you."

Her smile was sad, and moving her hand, she traced the lines of his jaw. "You can't promise that."

"I'm promising it anyway."

He was sweet, she thought, and he was sincere, whether Jason could see it or not. He'd told her, after all, that he couldn't read minds. Maybe his insight was biased. Maybe his warnings were steeped in jealousy. Maybe it was time she stopped looking back and concentrated instead on what lay ahead. Maybe the next time Jason appeared, she should close her eyes and refuse to see him.

And maybe not.

"So are you ready for your shower tomorrow night?" he asked, still fondling her hand.

"I guess."

"My mother's invited everyone she's ever known. I hope there's room for them all."

"Feels funny, having people I don't know giving me presents."

"Take 'em and run," Stephen said on a laugh. "My mother's given their children a fortune in gifts. It's her turn."

She smiled. "Seems like this is more your mother's wedding than mine."

"Be happy that she's taking such an interest. It takes a lot of pressure off of you."

"Does it?"

He shot her a sharp look. "Hey, come on. Don't be ungrateful."

"I'm not. I do appreciate everything she's done. I could never have pulled all this off without her."

"Judging by your pictures of your first wedding, I'd say your own parents couldn't have handled it. Financially or otherwise."

Something about his tone rankled her, and she gave him a hard look. "They did just fine when Jason and I got married. It wasn't a huge, elegant wedding, but it was beautiful and...very, very sweet. Besides, even if I'd needed the money, I would never have asked them to pay for a second one."

"Why not? That's what parents are for."

Again, her eyes hardened. "No, Steven. That's not what parents are for."

Sensing her chagrin, his expression sobered. "Hey, what's wrong?"

"Nothing," she said.

He reached for her hand and pulled her out of her chair, and reluctantly she got up and allowed him to pull her into his lap. He closed his arms around her and nuzzled his face against her neck. "You're not having cold feet, are you?"

She sighed. "Aren't you?"

"No," he whispered. "You're the best thing that's ever happened to me. I can't wait until you're my wife."

"Me, too," she said. "There's just so much to do. I'm a little overwhelmed."

"I know," he said. "Look, just tell me what you don't want to do, and I'll get my mother to do it."

A sly smile tugged at her lips. "How about going to the bridal shower, for starters?"

"Sorry, honey. You have to go to that."

"Yeah, I thought so."

She got off his lap and went across the kitchen to wash out the coffeepot. "So tell me," she said as matter-of-factly as she could. "Do your buddies plan to throw you some kind of wild bachelor party before the wedding?"

"Didn't I tell you?" he asked. "They're planning one for the night before the wedding."

She should have been happy that he had told the truth, but instead she felt strangely disappointed. "Hmm. And will there be dancing girls jumping out of cakes?"

He grinned. "I don't know. I'm just the guest of honor. But you have nothing to worry about. The only girl I'd be interested in seeing jump out of a cake would be you. I'll probably sneak out early and rest up for the wedding. What about you?"

She shrugged. "Anna's husband is going offshore that week, so she and Danny and I decided to get together that night with some of our old friends. Kind of like a last fling of the old gang."

For a moment, he didn't respond, and she turned to look at him, for she knew his silence spoke volumes.

"Are you sure you want to do that?"

"Well, yeah. Why not?"

"I don't know." His grave expression told her that *he* was sure he didn't want her to. "I just hope you don't plan to hang out with that guy after we're married. It would be scandalous."

"Scandalous? How?"

"Married women don't pal around with single men. It's just not right."

"Danny is one of my closest friends, Steven. I'm not going to turn my back on him just because I'm getting married."

He raised his hands in mock surrender and said, "Never mind. We'll talk about it later."

"Later when? After we're married? What are you going to do? Give me a list of rules as soon as the wedding ring is on my finger?"

"No, I'm not going to give you a list of rules. What's the matter with you? Are you just looking for something to fight about?"

She breathed out a heavy breath. "No. I just don't like having my friends chosen for me."

"Forget I ever said anything," he said. He got up and grabbed his briefcase. "I'm going home to change. Do you want me to come back later, or are you planning to still be in a foul mood?"

"That's up to you," she said.

"Right." He left her standing there, and she gritted her teeth as the door slammed behind him.

"Why didn't you ask him about a prenuptial agreement?"

Sabrina swung around and confronted Jason, who was leaning against the counter as if he belonged there and gazing at her with one eyebrow hiked up in that maddening way he had.

"Jason, you're going to scare me to death."

"I can think of worse things," he said. "Now why didn't you ask him?"

"I forgot," she said.

"Forgot? How could you forget? Don't you think that's important?"

"Of course I do, but it wasn't the right time. He was already hurt about the house."

"Hurt?" he said with a laugh. "That's a joke. The guy was shaking in his boots."

"His concerns are legitimate, Jason. What he said about my clinging to the past is true. He has a right to want me to leave my past behind." Throwing up her hands, she said, "And if he knew that I'm standing here talking to you . . ."

"Do you want me to quit coming?"

She wilted. "No."

"Because if that's really what you want, I will."

"I said no, Jason!"

"Why?"

"Because I—" Her voice broke, and all the fury was gone. All that was left was deep, unhealing sadness. "Because I love seeing you. But I feel like I'm losing my mind a little at a time, and I'm standing here listening to my dead husband analyze me and pretend to read my mind."

"Nope. I told you I can't read minds. But I can read you."

"Did you get the gift of divine wisdom when you went to heaven?"

As facetious as her question had been, Jason took it seriously. "Actually, no. They only give that when you blend fully into heaven. I haven't yet. They tell me that when I let go of my past I'll be given celestial understanding. I look forward to that. Then maybe I'll understand why such a beautiful woman with so much going for her would sell herself so short."

Sabrina turned away from him and leaned on the counter, dropping her head. "I don't know how much more of this I can take. You're making me feel so divided. So confused."

"You're confused because you're taking the wrong path, babe. That's why I'm here."

She took a deep, cleansing breath and turned to him, taking comfort in the sight of his face, his hair, the dark curls at his throat. "Jason, I know it hurts you to see me marrying someone else. I think part of the problem I'm having is that I feel disloyal to you. I feel guilty for falling in love again."

The pain in his eyes made her instantly sorry for being so blunt.

"Is that what you have for him, Bree? Love?"

"Yes," she said emphatically. "I couldn't marry him if I didn't."

Jason's face went slack as he gazed at her, and finally he whispered, "Don't love him, Bree. I don't want to see you get hurt."

"Jason, you're driving me crazy."

"I know it seems that way, but you're not going crazy, babe. You're as sane as I am."

"Gee, thanks."

He grinned and gazed quietly at her for a moment. "So have you told Danny about me?"

She shot him a look. "Don't you know?"

"Hey, I don't see everything, Bree. I can't be around all the time. They'd never allow that. Matter of fact, I have to fight really hard for the times they do let me come."

She tried to imagine Jason fighting heaven's city hall, and smiled. "No, I haven't told Danny. I don't want him thinking I'm nuts."

"He might," Jason admitted. "He's a skeptical bugger. When we were kids, he didn't believe a man had walked on the moon. His whole family was convinced that the first moon walk took place in a television studio."

Her smile faded. "He didn't believe you were dead," she whispered.

He sobered. "What do you mean?"

Her eyes saddened as she remembered the evening the woman from the medical examiner's office had knocked on her door and told her that there had been an accident. "After they told me you were killed," she said, her voice breaking, "I called Danny. He came right over, and they told him. But he said no, it couldn't have happened. He almost convinced me that the car had been stolen and that it was somebody else's body behind the wheel. But I knew.... I felt it in my heart. You were gone."

She wiped at the tears smudging her eyes, and Jason came closer and looked down at her. Blinking back the mist in his eyes, he said, "I'm so sorry, baby. If I could have spared you...if there were any way..."

"We got through it," she said. "Your mom invited Danny to sit with the family at the funeral. She knew he was hurting as badly as we were."

Jason raked a hand through his hair. "Who would have believed, when we were kids, that one of us would go like that? And darn it all, it had to be me."

She grinned. "Are you saying you would have preferred it was one of us?"

"Well, sure," he said. "Then I could have taken the pain. And you could have lived it up in heaven. It's really a terrific place."

"Then why do you keep coming back here?"

He sighed and looked at her as if she could never in a million years understand.

And yet she did.

"I need for you to be happy, Bree. I can't bear letting you go until you are."

"I'm going to be happy, Jason."

"Ask him, Bree. Ask him for a prenuptial agreement and see how he reacts."

She nodded. "Okay, I will. Tonight. That is, if he can stand coming around me. I've been such a shrew lately...."

"You've never been a shrew. Don't mistake your doubts for crankiness, Bree. Don't let anybody tell you it's just cold feet. And don't tell yourself."

Her head began to ache, and she closed her eyes. "Jason, if you really want me to be happy..." Her words trailed off, as though she couldn't bear to say them.

"What?" he prodded. "If I really wanted you to be happy, would I leave you alone?"

"No," she said too quickly. "I don't want you to leave me alone." Her eyes shone as she looked at him. "I love seeing you. Even if it means I'm going nuts. Please don't stop coming. Even after I'm married, you'll still come, won't you?"

Her question had a tinge of desperation to it, and he longed to touch her hair and press a kiss on her lips. But he knew better. Instead, he let his eyes caress her. "Baby, they won't let me keep coming forever. I'm here on a mission. If you get back on the right path, you won't need me. And if I fail and you marry Steven, well, even then, my job is over."

Tears streamed down her face, and she whispered, "You could keep coming for a while, Jason. Just to keep in touch. Just so I'd know..."

"It's not up to me, baby," he whispered. "It never was."

"But this is all so cruel!"

A tear seeped out of the corner of his eye. "You'll be happy if you listen to me, Bree. I know it doesn't seem like it, but you'll have a full, wonderful life, and all the things that are important to you will be yours."

"You won't!"

"My importance will fade," he whispered. "One day you won't be able to remember exactly what I look like, and you'll go entire weeks without thinking of me. You'll grow old with someone who adores you, and after a while, it'll seem like your only marriage. That is, if you marry the right person."

"You're wrong," she said weakly. "I've been waiting three years for the memory to fade, and it's grown so strong that I'm conjuring you up. It's only going to get worse."

"You couldn't conjure me if you wanted to," he whispered. "We mortals, we're not that powerful." He locked gazes with her, making her listen. "They let me come because you've been through enough pain. You need some grace and mercy. And that's in great supply in heaven. Do you trust me?"

"Yes," she whispered. "I trust you."

"Then you'll check out what I've said? You know, the sooner you discover Steven's ulterior motives and get out of this farce of a wedding, the sooner you can get on with the life that's planned for you."

"I don't want to doubt him," she whispered. "I want everything to be all right."

"It isn't going to be all right, babe. Not if you marry him. Trust me."

She looked in his eyes, and she could feel his warmth, as close as he could be without touching her. She caught his scent, that special combination of just-showered clean and outdoor maleness, and she realized that she'd give everything she'd ever owned to have one more moment in his arms.

His lips lowered to hers, and the look on his face told her he was tormented by what he was about to do. But somehow, he couldn't stop himself.

She closed her eyes, waiting for the moment of magic, the moment when she could taste him again, but it didn't happen. Finally, she opened her eyes.

Jason was gone.

STEVEN WAS CONCILIATORY when he returned that night with a bag of Chinese food and a bouquet of fresh-cut daisies. When she opened the door, he gave her a sweet look and said, "Are we still friends?"

She smiled and took the flowers. "If that's sweet and sour chicken, we are."

"Good," he said, leaning down to kiss her. "I don't like it when we fight. Let's not do it anymore."

"Okay." She hugged him tightly, feeling the old affection for him stirring in her heart, but some part of her was aware that Jason could be watching. A shiver went through her, and she pulled back. "Come on, let's eat."

They pulled the food out and got out plates, and the whole time, Jason's words kept going through her mind. *Ask him about a prenuptial agreement.* But she was afraid to disturb the good feelings he had brought over.

They were halfway through the meal when Steven cleared the way. "What's wrong, honey? There's something on your mind."

She sighed. "There's something I need to ask you. I just . . . I'm afraid it'll make you mad."

"I can take it," he said. "Go ahead."

She let out a deep breath. "I was just wondering how you would feel about a prenuptial agreement."

He dropped his fork. "A what? Sabrina, this isn't like you."

"Why not?"

"Because you're a traditionalist. You're old-fashioned. That's what I love about you. I can't believe you'd want such a thing."

"Why not? You have things of your own, I have things of my own. I would think you'd want to protect your interests."

He slid his chair back and got up, and she noted that his face was reddening by degrees. "This beats everything. I don't believe it."

"Why?"

"Because of the trust, Sabrina!" he shouted. "People who trust each other don't need prenuptial agreements."

For a moment she was quiet, for she knew that she'd always felt the same way about them. She and Jason had never discussed having one together, and if Steven had brought the subject up, she would probably have been offended. But that didn't mean she had any intentions of leaving him and taking whatever money he had. It didn't mean he planned to, either.

"I know it seems that way, Steven. But I do trust you. The prenuptial agreement is only in the event that trust is broken. If we keep our vows, it'll never be used."

"I'm going to keep my vows, Sabrina. Don't you plan to keep yours?"

"Of course I do. But good intentions go bad all the time. People always plan to keep their vows, and along the way something goes wrong. People change. We don't know what might happen."

"And you're afraid I'll try to get your money."

She sighed. "No, I'm not afraid of that at all."

He dropped his head and began massaging his temples. "I thought we discussed the fact that when we're married, what's yours is mine and what's mine is yours."

"Of course we did."

"Do you still agree with that?"

"Well . . . yes. In theory."

The vein in his temple began to throb. "In theory? What does that mean?"

She looked around, as if expecting Jason to be standing somewhere behind a door or the refrigerator, waiting to prompt her if she needed help. "I mean that you've been pretty pushy about the house. I'm having trouble selling it, Steven, and you've just bulldozed right past me, called Anna yourself, made arrangements for her to list it...."

"Oh, so that's what it's all about. It's a control thing."

"No, it's not a control thing!" She was getting angry, and she came to her feet and glared at him. "Steven, this house is worth a lot more than money to me. It's hard for me to let it go, but you're not showing any understanding."

"Hey, did I force you to set a date this soon? Am I twisting your arm into marrying me?"

She started to say no, as he expected her to, but some part of her resisted. "Actually, it *was* your idea to rush things."

"Rush things?" he shouted. "I thought you *wanted* to get married."

She wilted and sat down. "I do."

"Then what is it? What's this all about?"

She thought for a moment, trying to find words. "Steven, why did we choose the date we chose?"

"I don't know," he said. "Your birthday seemed like a good idea. You were so bummed about turning thirty. We decided it together."

"Not really. You chose, and I agreed. I was flattered that you were so anxious."

"But you're not flattered anymore, are you?" he accused. "Now you're mad because you weren't the one who chose."

She shook her head. "But it does seem like you're making all the decisions." She sighed and looked tentatively at him. "I feel like I'm going through some kind of out-of-body experience, and I'm watching myself being manipulated through some scene that I have no real part in."

He stared at her for a moment, and part of her prayed that he would melt and tell her how sorry he was, that she had him all wrong, that he loved her more than life itself and that he would do it her way—at least some of it—if it would ease her fears. But instead, he seemed to grow colder. "So I'm controlling and manipulating you into rushing the wedding. A wedding you're entering into with an escape hatch. Is that it?"

Anger grew thicker inside her. "That's not what I'm asking for. But I have to maintain a little autonomy."

"People with autonomy are generally alone, Sabrina. I think you'd better decide what it is you really want."

"I want a prenuptial agreement."

He stared at her, his face crimson, and she realized she'd never seen quite as much anger in his eyes. "I want to marry you, Sabrina, but if my vows aren't good enough for you, then maybe we should call it off.'' With that he slammed out of the house before she had a chance to stop him.

"Steven!" she shouted, half in fear, half in anger.

But she heard his car pulling out of the driveway, screeching as he shifted into gear.

Tears came to her eyes, and she shouted, "Are you happy, Jason?"

But Jason didn't answer. Her voice seemed loud against the night. The words were launched without impact, and fell back into her own heart.

She stared into the distance, at the wallpaper she and Jason had replaced together, noting the place where they'd run out and wound up splicing pieces at the bottom. No one had ever noticed it, but they had known, and finally they'd put a table in front of it to divert the eye. She wondered, if she sold it, what the next owners might do to this room.

And why did it matter so?

She cleaned up the remnants of their dinner and decided to go to bed, to curl up in her misery and contemplate what she had done. Would Steven be back, or was she right back at square one, alone with no one to love her, alone with nothing but the ghost of a man she couldn't touch, alone with a dismal future where there was nothing to look forward to?

Bed was a lonely place, a place where she thought of all the other couples across the world, snuggled up under the covers the way she and Jason used to do, finding so much comfort in the fact that there was a warm body who cared deeply lying just a fingertip's distance away.

She wanted that again.

But it wasn't Steven she thought of when she lay in bed at night, but Jason. She wondered if she'd think of him even after she was Steven's wife.

That is, if he still wanted to marry her after his anger festered all night. And she didn't blame him. She had implied that he was controlling her, that she didn't trust him, that she wanted guarantees. But there were no guarantees in marriage, and she knew that.

There's one guarantee, she told herself suddenly. *There's the guarantee that Jason knows something you don't know, and that he warned you Steven would react that way.* But wouldn't any man? It didn't take a genius to predict it would rub him the wrong way.

But the more Steven had resisted the idea of a prenuptial agreement, the more determined Sabrina had become to have one. Why was it so important when she knew it hurt him? Could it be that she really *didn't* trust him? Could it be that she really *didn't* know him well enough to marry him?

No. She was ready. She knew she was.

"What are you going to do if he says no?"

The voice from the darkness startled her, and she saw the shadow of her husband in the corner across the room. "Jason, couldn't you start coming through a door? Knock or something?"

He only crossed his arms and leaned against the wall. "Still sleeping in my shirts, hey?"

She let out a weary breath. "I asked him, just like you told me to. And he reacted just like you predicted."

"Then answer my question. What are you going to do when he says no?"

"I don't know," she said.

For a moment he was quiet. "And what are you going to do about the house?"

She sat up, pulled her legs up under the covers and hugged her knees. "What do you think I should do?"

"I think you should follow your heart, baby. It's served you pretty well before."

"Not always," she whispered.

In the shadows, she saw his brows come together. Those perfect, full, satiny brows. "When hasn't it?"

"When I fell in love with you."

Her words hurt him, and she was sorry she'd said them. But there seemed no room for anything less than honesty between them.

"You're sorry for that?"

Her words took almost more effort than she could manage. "I wish I could have fallen just as deeply in love with someone who would have been around forever."

"Nobody will be around forever, baby. Everybody has to go sometime."

"But I could have had more time to be happy. Just a little more time."

"Your happy days aren't over, babe."

She tried to smile. "I wish I had your faith."

"Well, faith is a little easier from this side."

He came toward her and urged her to lie down. Her head fell into the pillows, and he pulled the covers up around her, tucking her in.

"Remember when we used to cuddle in the mornings?" she whispered. "And sometimes, in the middle of the night, if you woke up you'd pull me next to you and hold me."

"I remember," he whispered.

She sighed, and a tear rolled out of her eye. "I want that again, Jason. This bed gets so lonely."

"It can be just as lonely with the wrong person."

"I know." She looked at him through the blur of her tears. "Are you sure he's the wrong guy, Jason? You wouldn't jerk me around, would you?"

"Baby, what would I have to gain? All I want is for you to be happy."

"I know." She closed her eyes, wishing the tears would go away, wishing sleep would come and heal all the aches of her lonely soul.

"Go to sleep," he whispered.

"Will you stay, Jason?" she asked. "Just until I fall asleep?"

"I'll be here. Close your eyes." She closed her eyes, and even though he couldn't touch her, she felt his presence, warm and comforting, just a fingertip's distance away. Someone loved her. Someone protected her. Someone watched over her.

And Sabrina fell into the deepest sleep she'd had since she'd last slept with Jason.

Chapter Four

Steven arrived on schedule the next morning—just as if the argument hadn't occurred. But the fact that he had his mother in tow—so she could brief Sabrina on the guests she'd invited to the shower Anna was giving that night—made it difficult to talk.

"Steven, could I speak to you in the kitchen for a minute?" Sabrina asked pleasantly, turning on the television so that his mother wouldn't hear them.

He looked reluctant, but acquiesced.

Sabrina led him into the kitchen, then leaned against the counter, crossing her arms. "Steven, you slammed out of here in a fit last night. Why are you acting like nothing ever happened?"

"I missed you, that's why." His eyes were tired, as if he hadn't slept, and she felt a surge of guilt that she had. "Sabrina, I don't want to fight with you."

"Then you'll sign the prenuptial agreement?"

He sighed and pulled her against him and stroked her hair. "We'll talk about it some more," he said. "But it's not worth breaking up over. I love you."

"I love you, too," she whispered, though the words seemed more strained than they had before.

"I really have to go now," he said. "I have an appointment. But I'll be back tonight after the shower, okay?"

"Okay," she said.

He kissed her then, a sweet, long, tender kiss, but her pulse didn't respond the way it should have. "You'd better go," she whispered.

She saw him to the door, then took a deep breath and faced his mother.

"Is everything all right with you two?" Elaine asked.

"Sure. It's fine." But everything wasn't really fine. Her heart was no longer at peace with this marriage—if it had ever been at all.

But the day swept her into a whirlwind of plans and activities that only got her more deeply entrenched in it. And that night, as she sat in Anna's home surrounded by women chattering about how she'd finally "found someone," she realized there was a point past which she could not get out of her plans—and she had crossed it.

"Honey, what's the matter with you?" her mother asked her when she got her alone in the kitchen. "You're practically moping."

She sighed. "I don't know, Mom. It's just too much. I can't take it all in."

"Did you and Steven have a fight?"

"A little one. And it wasn't exactly resolved."

Her mother, who had always been a good friend to her and had a special gift of reacting without passing judgment, set her arm around Sabrina's shoulders. "Are you worried about it?"

"It was important to me, Mom. I wish we could have finished talking about it before I came here."

"Will it make a difference in your plans?"

Sabrina honestly didn't want to tell her mother that she was accepting fifty gifts tonight and still wasn't certain she was going through with the wedding. "No, not really."

"Then smile," her mother said. "Things seem really big when we're under stress. Calm down and try to enjoy the attention. After the wedding you'll look back and wish you had."

Sabrina hugged her mother and pressed a kiss on her cheek. "I know. Thanks, Mom."

The kitchen door swung open, and Elaine fluttered in. "Really, darling, you've got to get back in there. We don't want to be rude now, especially when they've brought you such nice things."

Sabrina's smile faded. "No, of course not."

"Then go, go, go," her future mother-in-law said, herding them toward the door. "It's time to open gifts."

The doorbell rang, and Sabrina blew her bangs back from her face. "I thought everyone I've ever known was already here. Who could it be?"

"I'll get it," Anna cried, pushing through the guests, more than she'd ever expected to have to fit into her home, and opened the door.

Jason's mother stood timidly on the porch, smiling past Anna at Sabrina.

Suddenly, something came alive inside her, and she bolted forward. "Leigh Ann! I'm so glad you came." She threw her arms around her mother-in-law, the woman who'd been so good to her since she lost her son.

Leigh Ann pulled back and touched Sabrina's face tenderly. Her eyes were so like Jason's that Sabrina found herself wanting to gaze into them. "I wouldn't have missed it for the world."

"Well, aren't you going to introduce me?" Elaine prompted, and Sabrina turned around.

"Yes, of course. Leigh Ann Hill, this is Steven's mother, Elaine. Leigh Ann is my mother-in-law."

The fact that she referred to her status in the present tense made Elaine's smile falter somewhat, and she offered a pseudo-gracious handshake. "We're so glad you could come. Really. But a few moments later, and you would have missed the gift opening."

Sabrina felt the sting of Elaine's reprimand, and thought how funny it was that the woman was so concerned with not being rude but managed to be so every time she opened her mouth. Sabrina looked at Leigh Ann and noted the strain on her face. It had been hard for her to come, she thought. In fact, her mother-in-law had probably changed her mind a dozen times. But she truly wanted to see Sabrina happy. She had come out of love.

Sabrina took the seat they had chosen for her, and she pulled Leigh Ann with her. As the other guests began to sit down, Leigh Ann leaned toward her.

"Honey, I've got something for you in the car, but I'd rather give it to you alone. Can you save a few minutes for me after the shower?"

Sabrina smiled and wished from her heart that she could tell her about all the times she'd seen Jason in the last few days, that he looked better than ever and that he'd started a little coalition of heavyweights in heaven worrying about him and making special concessions to him. It had always happened wherever Jason went, and she was sure his mother would enjoy it.

But chances were, she wouldn't believe a word.

She began opening presents, overreacting to each one just as Elaine would have dictated, and by the time she'd opened half she fought the urge to tell them that was enough, and that she'd open the rest tomorrow. But that would have been ungrateful, she thought. This was supposed to be fun.

She was exhausted by the time all the presents had been opened and all the guests had left, but when she saw Anna and Leigh Ann and her own mother talking in the corner, she remembered what Jason's mother had said. Excusing herself from the last of Elaine's guests, she joined them.

"It was a wonderful shower, Anna," she said. "Thank you."

Anna gave her a worried look. "Are you sure you're okay? You seem a little stressed out."

"Wouldn't you be?" She tried to laugh, then took Leigh Ann's hands. "Was this okay for you, Leigh Ann?"

Leigh Ann only laughed softly. "Honey, the thought of you being happy again just does wonders for me. Please believe that."

"I do," she whispered.

Leigh Ann squeezed her hand. "Do you have a minute now, to walk out to the car with me?"

"Sure, I do," she said.

They held hands and walked the short distance down the street to where Jason's mother had parked. "You look radiant," Leigh Ann said. "It brings back a lot of memories."

"For me, too," Sabrina said.

They reached the car, and Leigh Ann stopped, turned to her and looked out over the street. "Before Jason died," she whispered, "I'd been planning to give you something that was very special in our family. Something that's traditionally passed down through the generations. But I'm afraid there's no one left to pass it to, since Jason died. So I've decided to give it to you."

Sabrina frowned as Leigh Ann reached into the car and pulled out a big wrapped gift that seemed difficult for her to lift. "Open it here," Leigh Ann said.

Sabrina tore into the paper, reached the unmarked box underneath and opened it. Her face was pale as she saw what was inside. "Oh, Leigh Ann," she whispered. "It's your silver set." She caught a breath and shook her head. "I can't take this. It's been in your family for ten generations."

"Eleven. But it's yours now."

Tears ambushed her from out of nowhere, and she felt a tremendous sadness at the sweet gesture. "Oh, Leigh Ann. This is the sweetest thing.... I'm just not sure... I don't know..."

"What, dear?"

If this marriage is worthy of this, she almost said, but she caught herself. "You've been so good to me," she told her instead. "And I love you so much. And just because I'm remarrying, it doesn't mean that you won't still be my mother-in-law. And it doesn't mean that I'll ever forget Jason."

"Oh, I know that, sweetheart." She hugged her, a hug so tight and warm it gave Sabrina the sustenance she needed to go back into Anna's house.

"But isn't there a cousin or niece, someone still in the family that you could give this to?"

"No," Leigh Ann said firmly. "I'm giving it to you."

Sabrina wiped at the tears on her face. "Thank you."

Leigh Ann wiped her own eyes and took a deep breath. "Now you get back in there and start packing up those gifts. It'll take you all night to get them home."

Sabrina nodded as her mother-in-law got into the car.

"I'll see you at the wedding, okay?" Leigh Ann asked her.

Sabrina hesitated. "Are you sure?"

"I'll sleep better that night, knowing you're well taken care of," she said. "I want to be there."

Sabrina held the box with the family's most treasured heirloom and watched as Jason's mother drove away. And then, when she was out of her sight, she fought the urge to get in her car, leave all those gifts behind and go home with only that one gift. The gift that meant the most to her.

The gift of Jason's mother's support.

INSTEAD OF JASON, it was Steven who waited for her at home, ready to carry all the gifts in and examine them.

"Did you get anything good?" he asked, going through her trunk and back seat with eyes as big as a kid's on Christmas morning.

"Everything I got was good." She lifted the box of silver and started to her door.

"Here, I'll get that. It looks heavy."

"No, that's okay. I've got it." Ashamed of herself for not wanting him to touch it, she took it into the house and set it down on her dining room table. As Steven made several trips in and out to unload the car, she opened the box and pulled out each piece in turn. She had always loved Jason's family's silver set, but it had never occurred to her that it would someday be hers. She thought of all of Jason's ancestors who had sipped tea from it, and a surge of warmth went through her.

"What's that?" Steven was out of breath when he came to her side.

"A silver set," she said, smiling at the fact that Leigh Ann had even polished it for her. "Isn't it beautiful?"

"Who in the world gave us that?" Steven asked. "It's worth a fortune."

"It's worth a lot more than money," she said. "It's from Jason's mother."

For a moment, he looked crestfallen, but then he brightened. "Good Lord, this is fantastic. Is there a registration certificate or anything?"

She frowned at him. "What do you mean?"

"Well, I mean that most gifts come with some kind of registration. Some of these things are collectors' items, and others have certificates, that kind of thing. Was there anything with this?"

"Steven, it's been in the family for eleven generations. I'm not real concerned about paperwork."

"Well, I guess that's all right," he said. "But we need to send the other cards in right away." He began opening boxes and pulling out paperwork. "I'll just gather them and put them in our safety deposit box before they get lost."

"Fine," she whispered.

He began commenting on each gift and the person who'd given it to them, and she sat quietly, still fingering the silver. She wondered what it would have been like if Leigh Ann had given it to her and Jason for their anniversary, if he had lived. Wouldn't it have been a great anniversary gift? Jason would have loved it.

"Looks like I've got all of them," Steven said. "Oh, by the way, while I'm getting all this anyway, why don't you give me the paperwork for your CDs? I'll just put those in the box, too."

Startled, she turned around. "Why?"

"Well, I don't want them to get lost in the move, darling. I might as well keep everything together and safe."

She remembered what Jason had said about her CDs, and a shiver went through her. "I don't have them here. Besides, it's almost time to reinvest them. I'll just take care of that first."

He looked disturbed, but tried to hide it. "Fine. I just thought you might want to talk about how to reinvest them. There are better ways, you know."

"Not safer ways."

"Hey, you're marrying a terrific stockbroker, darling. I wouldn't lead you wrong. Besides, after we're married, it'll all go into one pot. It'll be my money, too, and I wouldn't be stupid enough to lose that kind of money."

One pot. She knew Jason was listening from wherever he was, and that his ire was rising just as hers was. "I've made pretty good decisions about my money so far, Steven."

"Well, you don't have to make them anymore. That's my department. Get the paperwork for me tomorrow, and I'll put them in the box."

She was silent for a moment, and finally she decided that there was no use waiting any longer. "Steven, we haven't resolved the issue of the prenuptial agreement."

Steven groaned. "Oh, come on, Sabrina. You can't still be serious."

"I am."

"Fine," he said. "Then I should tell you that I talked to my lawyer today and he said there's no way he can get one drawn up within a week. The wedding is in seven days, Sabrina."

"I'm sure Danny could do it for us. I'd prefer that he did, anyway. I trust him."

"Danny?" he repeated. "Well, maybe he could, Sabrina, but there's no way I'm going to let your ex-husband's law partner draw up my prenuptial agreement."

"Jason is not my ex-husband," she threw back. "We didn't divorce. He was still my husband—"

"He died, Sabrina! It's till death do you part."

"That's a matter of opinion." The moment the words were out of her mouth, she knew she had gone too far.

"You can't have two husbands, Sabrina. I suggest you decide whether you want to hang on to a memory or embrace the present."

Sabrina almost faltered, but her head was amazingly clear. "This conversation is not about my memories, Steven."

His face hardened. "Sabrina, I think you've been under too much stress, and I don't know who's been filling your head with these ideas, but I have to tell you that it's making me real uneasy."

"It doesn't have to," she said. "Just sign the agreement and we never have to think about it again."

"And if I don't?"

So it had come to that, she thought. An ultimatum. And she was going to have to mean it.

"If you don't, I won't marry you."

His face fell. "What?"

"You heard me, Steven."

He was dumbfounded, and as he gaped at her, she wondered if she was being unreasonable. She was quite sure Jason would have told her she wasn't.

"You would break our engagement, call this whole thing off, over a piece of paper?"

"It's important to me," she said.

"But you can't back out now," he said through compressed lips. "There are plans, Sabrina. A church, a dress, airline tickets, guests...and all these gifts!"

"I'll send them back. It won't be easy, but I can do it."

"Sabrina, do you have any idea how much money has been spent on this wedding already?"

"I never wanted to spend a lot of money," she said. "But sacrifices have to be made sometimes for getting one's head clear."

"Your head is anything but clear. You're in a cloud, Sabrina. You're losing it!"

"Maybe so." She took off the engagement ring he had given her, the one her friends had been so envious of, the one that had been twice as big as Jason's, but half as special.

"Here," she said as tears came to her eyes—not tears for Steven, but tears for the hopes she'd had of having a family, the dreams of having someone lie next to her each night, the fulfillment of knowing she would never have to be alone again. But those were empty dreams, she thought, for there were no guarantees with Steven. Only doubts.

He took the ring, amazed that she would go this far, and finally he got to his feet. "I think we both need some time alone," he said, his voice rippling with restrained anger. "And I especially think that you need to think about what you're doing. Think about what you're throwing away."

She nodded, feeling a more profound sense of relief than she would have ever expected. "I'm sorry, Steven."

"Sorry," he repeated bitterly. "Yeah. I think you're gonna be sorry."

Then he stalked from the house, and in the depths of her heart, Sabrina knew he wouldn't be back.

"Way to go, baby."

She wasn't surprised to hear Jason's voice, and her anger only escalated, as fresh, despairing tears began to sluice down her cheeks. Covering her face, she cried, "Shut up, Jason."

He flinched. "Hey, you've never said that to me before."

"You've never ruined my life before."

He hadn't expected sobs, and frustrated, he stepped closer, wishing he could touch her, comfort her. "I didn't ruin your life, baby. I was trying to save it."

"Yeah, well, who asked for your help?"

Stalking from the room, she took the stairs two at a time until she was in her bedroom. Jason followed her all the way. "What is it, Bree? Talk to me!"

Her face was raging red and wet as she turned to him. "What if I loved him, Jason? What if I truly, deeply wanted to marry him?"

"You were marrying him by default, Bree, and you know it! You thought he was your last chance, and you were wrong. Besides, I didn't force you to break up. I only told you what you needed to know. You made the decision."

"But I didn't have to know!" she cried. "I could have been happily oblivious, Jason. Just like I was when I was married to you!"

"Oblivious to what?"

"Oblivious to the fact that you were going to leave me and put me through all this." Her hand came out and knocked over a bottle of perfume sitting on the dresser, and it crashed to the floor. She left the shattered pieces there, and collapsed onto her bed, covering her face.

"I never left you intentionally," he said, his voice as quiet as hers had been loud. "And I'm still here, aren't I? When you need me?"

"Are you going to be here tomorrow when I start sending those gifts back, and when I start to realize just how alone I am, and that there's nothing in my life to look forward to except a lot more days alone? No babies, no husband, no plans. Just a bunch of stupid memories?"

"Our memories are not stupid."

The pain in his voice seemed to heighten her pain, and unable to make sense of any of it anymore, she lay down on the bed and buried her face in the pillow, weeping out all the anger and blame and bitterness she had carried with her since the day Jason dropped out of her life. She felt the mattress move as he sat down next to her, and as if he touched her without making physical contact, she felt a sweet warmth caress her hair. Turning onto her side, she looked at him. His hand hovered over her, not touching, and his eyes welled with tears of his own. She sucked in another sob, dying to throw her arms around him, but that was the greatest irony of all. That she couldn't. That he was here, to see and love and not touch.

His irony was that this was worse than the death that had taken him away in the first place. It had been instant, painless, but this was a slow death, for it was hers. If only she could have been taken, and he could have been the one left behind. He could endure the pain, just knowing that she was in a better, safer place, where her heart wasn't likely to be broken again. But instead, he was where he was, and she was left behind, and each time he saw her, some new part of him died all over again.

Her anger seemed to have drained, along with her energy, and exhausted from the extent of her anguish, she looked at him through wet lashes. "She gave me the silver set. It was the sweetest thing."

"Mom's like that. She always intended to give it to you, you know."

"She intended to give it to us, Jason. Not me. Us."

"Still . . ."

"But there won't be any babies for me to pass it down to," she said weakly. "It stops here, doesn't it, Jason?"

"No, baby. It doesn't stop here. This is where it starts. Now you're open to the right plan."

"There is no plan, is there, Jason? Isn't that just something we dangle in front of our own noses, to give us a reason to go on?"

"Absolutely not," he said. "There's a plan, Bree. You're going to fall in love with the right guy. And you'll be so happy."

"I'm not going to fall in love with Danny," she said. "I can't."

"Yes, you can," he said. "You'll see. And the two of you will have a houseful of kids, and you'll laugh all the time."

"What will happen to you?" she whispered.

"I'll stop coming, baby, so that you can be happy. And I'll be happy in heaven, and when they see that I've become a part of it all, I'll start to understand all the things I never understood before . . . like why I always used to feel guilty for locking my car doors when a shady-looking character was standing on the curb, or who 'they' are in the infamous 'they say.'"

"They're a committee of twelve scientists at the Centers for Disease Control in Atlanta," she said, sniffing.

He frowned. "What? Who told you that?"

"Danny," she said with a grin. "He figured it out."

Jason threw his head back and laughed, and slowly, Sabrina started to chuckle, too. "That sounds like Danny."

"Yeah, it does, doesn't it?"

They laughed some more, and finally, Sabrina's laughter faded on a sigh.

"You see? I told you he could make you laugh."

"He does, Jason. But that doesn't mean we have a life together."

"Give it a chance," he said. "And you might have to make the first move. He's a pretty loyal friend, that guy."

"Jason, I can't do that."

"Then just tell him that I was here and what I said."

Again, she found herself laughing. "Right. I'm supposed to tell Danny that I've been consulting with the ghost of my husband, who's told me that the two of us are supposed to get married and have babies."

"Not like that. But I'm telling you, you have to make a move."

"Why don't you go to him and tell him?"

"Because they won't let me show myself to anyone but you. It's up to you, babe."

She couldn't stop laughing, and finally, she realized that she was indeed losing her grip. "Do you think they put straitjackets on every insane person who has herself committed?"

"You're not insane, baby. Just hold on. All this will be so clear someday."

She looked at him for a moment as her laughter faded, and she whispered, "Thank you, Jason. I know you were right about Steven."

"Then you won't let him talk you into coming back tomorrow?"

"No. It's done. You were right."

"Then call Danny," he whispered. "Right now. He's your best friend. You would have called him anyway, if it weren't for me. Either him or Anna, but after all Anna's been through for you tonight, you'd probably be wise to wait until tomorrow to tell her."

She nodded.

He kissed his fingertips, then moved them to within a milimeter of her lips. But he didn't touch her. "I'll go now," he said, "so you can have some privacy with him. But I'll be back."

Her eyes grew wide with incipient tears as he walked out of her room, just like anyone else would have walked out. But she knew he didn't go where anyone else went.

Slowly, she picked up the phone and dialed.

DANNY'S PHONE startled him when it rang, and he dropped the footrest on his recliner, grabbed the remote control to turn down David Letterman and reached for the phone.

"Hello?"

"Hi, Danny. It's me."

Something about Sabrina's voice always made him smile, and pleased that she had called, he cut the television off altogether. "Hey, kiddo. How'd the shower go?"

"Great," she said.

"Were there a lot of people there?"

"Yeah. Too many."

"Did you get a lot of stuff?"

"Yeah. Too much."

Something about her tone sent an alarm ringing in his head, and he frowned and came to his feet. "What's wrong?"

"Um...well, Steven and I have... We've kind of...decided to call the wedding off."

Something leapt in Danny's heart, and his eyebrows shot up. "Why?"

"I don't know, Danny," she whispered. "Something just told me that he wasn't being straight with me...that maybe my money was playing a little more importance in this wedding than it should have."

"Hey, honey, look here. You're a beautiful, intelligent, sexy woman, and you don't need money to make a man fall in love with you. Steven had a prize on his hands, and I'm sure he knew it."

"No, Danny, I don't think so. I asked him for a prenuptial agreement, and he absolutely refused to sign it."

Danny sat down. "Do you want me to beat him up for you?"

She laughed. "No, I don't think so."

"I will, you know. I don't like seeing my friends with broken hearts. Especially you." His voice grew softer, more serious. "Are you sure you're all right?"

"Yeah, I am," she said. "As a matter of fact, I'm better than I've been in a long time. I'm gonna be fine, Danny."

"Look, I'm gonna come over there. We can talk, and—"

"No," she cut in. "It's late, and really, I'm fine. I'm tired, though, and tomorrow I have all these gifts to return, and a lot of stuff to cancel."

"I'll help you," he said. "I'll come over as soon as I get off work. And remember, it isn't crucial that you take care of everything in one day."

"I know," she said. "But the sooner, the better. I'll talk to you tomorrow, okay?"

"Okay," he said softly. "Be happy, all right?"

"All right. Good night, Danny."

When Danny hung up, he had a tentative smile on his face and a thousand thoughts racing through his mind, none of which he was certain he should be entertaining right now.

All he knew for sure was that he looked forward to seeing her tomorrow, without the pall of that wedding hanging over their heads.

Chapter Five

The sound from the angelic choir performing from the cloudy stage in the rainbow-colored sky was more upbeat than the Rolling Stones, more peaceful than Pachelbel, more emotional than Conway Twitty. It excited the heart even while it soothed it, and made Jason question why it wasn't enough for him.

But as mesmerizing as the choir was as it sang the songs Dave had written for them to perform, Jason still found himself distracted. Part of his heart still clung to Sabrina, and part of his mind still worried about her plight.

Breaking up with Steven was only a start. What if she didn't make a move on Danny, and her fears came true? What if she never found real happiness again? What if she was alone for the rest of her life?

He strolled through the throng of people on the golden streets, noting the serene and smiling faces, the camaraderie among everyone there, the warmth and acceptance. Too bad they couldn't get the hang of that on earth, he thought. He didn't know many of them, except for a handful of relatives, his father who kept real busy with deep-sea fishing, and the few people involved in trying to make him happy. He'd had ample opportunity to get to know lots of others since he'd been here, but he hadn't had much interest in making friends. He supposed he wouldn't until he let go of his old life completely and gave himself wholly to his surroundings.

"Hey, Jason, how's it goin', man?" Jason looked up and saw Peter ambling toward him, with a cute little blonde at his side. What the heck, he mused. The man probably deserved her.

"Hey, Pete," he said, shaking his hand. "Dave's choir is better than ever, isn't it?"

Peter took off his John Lennon glasses and gazed at the choir as they launched into the latest tune. "Sure is. He wrote that last night." Moving his eyes to Jason, he said, "Hey, I hear congratulations are in order. You accomplished your mission."

An alarm went off in Jason's chest, and with it came the stark fear that they would decide he'd done enough, that he could never go back. "Uh, well, not really. I mean, she broke up with him and all. But he'll be doing everything he can to win her back. And I have to get her pointed to Danny. She's pretty stubborn, sometimes."

Peter's face fell. "Jason, you can't direct her life. You have to let go."

"I will," he assured him. "When I'm sure."

Peter sighed. "Well, we should schedule you another meeting so we can decide how to proceed. I'll be in touch sometime today."

"Yeah, sure," Jason said.

"Meanwhile..." Peter's grin returned, and he set his arm across the shoulders of the little blond angel with the bright blue eyes and the smile that could have lit up a room on the other side. "Jason, I'd like for you to meet Rachel. She's just recently joined us. Worked as a nun in Spain. We're very proud of her here."

Jason smiled. "Hi, Rachel. How do you like it here so far?"

"It's more than I ever dreamed," she said zealously, looking around. "So wonderful. Have you been here long?"

"Time is relative here," Peter said. "We don't measure it the same way as you did on earth."

"Of course," Rachel said.

Peter nudged the woman forward and said, "Jason, why don't you show Rachel around? She hasn't yet seen the waters or the gardens."

Jason tried to tell Peter with his eyes that he wasn't interested. "As a matter of fact, I was just on my way somewhere. I sort of had an appointment."

One of Peter's eyebrows shot up, and Jason knew he wasn't pleased. "An appointment?"

"Yeah," Jason said, grasping. "For baseball tryouts."

"Baseball tryouts?" Peter asked. "Are you thinking about playing?"

Jason knew better than to lie, so he shook his head. "No, not me. I just thought I'd watch some of the players trying out for the team. I used to have this secret fantasy of playing third base in the pros. It's fun to watch, anyway."

"I see," Peter said, hope lighting his eyes again. "Well, then, you go on ahead. I'll find someone else to be Rachel's tour guide."

Jason nodded to the new angel and started away, not having any idea where the baseball clinic was being held, since he hadn't even thought of going until now. But he wasn't interested in being fixed up, he thought. He should have known. Now that they thought his mission was accomplished, they'd stoop as low as trying to get him interested in some angelic little ex-nun to get his mind off Sabrina.

If only it could be that easy.

ANNA DIDN'T SEEM surprised when Sabrina broke the news to her the next morning, and instead of preaching and judging—or screaming that she could have saved herself the time and effort it took to put that shower together—she took the day off work to help Sabrina return all the gifts.

She sat on the floor with her hair pulled back in a ponytail, a marking pen in one hand and a roll of packing tape in the other.

"I've known for the past couple of weeks that things weren't right," she said, sealing a box that would have to be mailed back since it came from one of Elaine's friends. "I mean, your reaction to my bringing the For Sale sign over was telling enough. Danny and I even talked about it."

"Danny?" Sabrina looked up from the apology cards she wrote. "What did he say?"

"He was worried about you. Wasn't sure you were doing the right thing."

"Why didn't either of you tell me?"

"We love you," Anna said. "We wanted to see you happy. But if you remember, we both tried to tell you not to rush."

Sabrina groaned and rubbed her temples. "I don't suppose I've been the most receptive person since we got engaged. I set that date, put on my blinders and barreled through like a fiend with a mission."

"You were receptive enough," Anna said. "You broke up with him, didn't you?" Returning to the table, she sat beside Sabrina. "Are you sure you're all right?"

"Yeah." She rested her chin on her palm. "I just feel kind of empty."

"There are worse feelings." Anna reached across the table and squeezed her hand. "I really do think you did the right thing."

Sabrina heard a car pulling into her driveway and with a wince she peered through the window. "Oh, no. It's Steven's mother."

"You want me to waylay her at the door? I could distract her long enough for you to ambush her from behind."

Sabrina grinned and got to her feet. "No, I might as well get it over with. But have the frying pan ready in case *she* attacks *me*." She looked around for the gift Elaine had given them last night, pulled it apart from the rest and headed for the door. As she went, she finger-brushed her loose hair and straightened the oversize shirt she wore with its tail out. Then, realizing that she no longer needed the woman's approval, she messed her hair up again and answered the door.

Elaine greeted her with thin, tight lips and a venomous look that warned she could be dangerous today.

"Hi, Elaine," Sabrina said.

Not answering, Elaine clomped in, holding her purse in the crook of her elbow. "I've come to get the gifts my friends and relatives had the misfortune of giving you last night," she said. "You know that it wouldn't be ethical for you to keep them."

"I had no intention of keeping them," Sabrina said. "In fact, I'm in the process of returning them all right now. But it would be a tremendous load off my mind if you *would* return some."

"I'm not interested in relieving your mind of its load," Elaine quipped. "But out of respect for my friends and family, I certainly will take what they gave you." As she spoke, Elaine walked into the kitchen where the gifts covered the counters and floor, and without speaking to Anna, began to stack those she recognized. "I can't imagine why you'd wait until after the shower to pick a fight with my son. You certainly could have saved us all a lot of trouble."

"I didn't plan it, Elaine."

"You know," the woman said, pivoting to face Sabrina, "you don't know how lucky you were to have been engaged to my son, and I'm sure you'll regret this decision one day. Steven is well-bred and intelligent, and he would have been an excellent husband to you."

"I know that," Sabrina said. "This was a personal decision."

Elaine fixed her with that angry, bitter stare, then turned to the gifts and began gathering them in her arms. "He'll find someone else, you know. He's a wonderful catch. Before you know it, you'll hear of him marrying someone else. How will you feel then?"

"I'll be glad that he found someone to make him happy," she said sincerely.

"It'll be too late for you then, you know."

"I can live with that."

Muttering a curse under her breath, Elaine marched to the door. "Then I suggest you start carrying some more of these to my car. I'll try to offer explanations personally, to make sure it's done right. But there is really no explanation for self-centered rudeness and insensitivity, is there?"

"No," Sabrina agreed, darting a look at Anna, who ducked her head to hide her amusement. "There really isn't."

They loaded all of Elaine's friends', relatives' and cohorts' presents into the car, and after the woman had screeched away, Anna shot Sabrina a look. "You know, she's going to trash you all over town."

"That's fine," Sabrina said. "We don't travel in the same circles, anyway."

Anna grinned. "But didn't it feel good? Finally not having to kowtow to her?"

"Yes," Sabrina said as she went inside. "It felt great. I think all this just might be worth it."

DANNY HEARD Sabrina's laughter in the kitchen when he came around to her back door late that afternoon. A tiny fear shot through him that Steven was back, that he had talked her out of breaking up and that they were going ahead with the wedding.

But when she opened the door, he saw only Anna there with her.

"And here I was afraid that you were moping around all day. I hurried over after work, determined that I was gonna be the one to cheer you up."

Sabrina pulled him into the kitchen. "Actually, we were laughing at some of the gifts we're returning." She reached into a box and pulled out a planter in the shape of a witch's head. "Can you imagine anyone giving me this?"

"And look at this," Anna said, brandishing another gift. "We think this is a sculpture of an elephant, but we're not sure. We know they'll be glad to get it back."

He took the odd-shaped sculpture and tried scratching his back with what appeared to be the trunk. "Don't you know a back scratcher when you see one? It also doubles as a shoe rest. You hang one on each ear. I have one in every closet."

On a laugh, Anna said, "I've got to go now. Mike'll be home soon. You guys gonna watch the meteor shower tonight?"

Danny shrugged. "I thought about driving the pickup out to the country and watching it. Wanna come, Sabrina?"

Sabrina was surprised at the sudden feeling of awkwardness that came over her. Before Jason had told her of "the plan," Danny's invitation would have seemed as natural as going with Anna. But things seemed different now. "Sure," she said. "That'll be fun."

"We can get a bite to eat before it turns dark," he said. "How about Italian?"

"Great." Smiling, she leaned against the counter, looking at both friends. "It's kind of good having my time all to myself again."

Danny grinned. "Yeah, I was just feeling a little guilty for being glad you're free to do stuff with me again."

A moment of silence passed between them, a moment that felt like chemistry. Almost.

"You sure you're okay?" Danny asked quietly.

She smiled. "I'm getting better all the time."

A FEW MINUTES LATER, she ran upstairs to change for dinner while Danny waited downstairs. She grabbed the first ironed thing she could find in her closet—a pair of khaki pants and a white oxford shirt—and started pulling her shirt off over her head.

"You're not wearing that, are you?"

She had almost stopped jumping when Jason appeared, but once again, he took her by surprise. "Jason!" She spun around and confronted him, lying on the bed with his hands behind his head, grinning that grin that probably should have kept him out of heaven.

Slowly, his grin faded as he sat up, his eyes sweeping her with a hungry longing. "I had almost forgotten how crazy you could make me." His eyes dropped to her jeans. Nodding toward them, he said, "Don't you need to take those off, too?"

Smiling, she unzipped them and slowly peeled them down her thighs, watching his reaction as she revealed the lacy bikini panties she wore, and thrilling in the fact that she still had the power to mesmerize him. Stepping out of the jeans, she asked, "Do they let you lust after women in heaven?"

He breathed a laugh. "You're still my wife, you know. There's nothing sinful about a man lusting for his wife."

"But it's till death do us part, Jason."

"Do I look dead?" he asked with a smile. "Whoever coined that till death do us part phrase never considered the afterlife. And yes, I still lust after you. We were real good together, Bree."

His breath had grown more labored, and for the most fleeting of moments, he considered what might happen if he reached out and touched that soft skin at her waist, rose to trace the shape of her breasts.... Would they pull him back before his hand had even made contact? Would they revoke his privileges to come here at all?

Moaning, he got up and went to look out the window, putting his back to her. Taking a deep, cleansing breath, he said, "Maybe this wasn't such a good idea, after all."

"I can get dressed," she whispered.

He nodded. "Yeah. Maybe you'd better."

He heard the clothes rustling behind him as she slipped on her blouse, and suddenly he remembered what he'd meant to tell her. Turning around, he asked, "You're not really going to wear that, are you?"

She looked down at the pants lying over a chair. "Well, why not? Danny's waiting downstairs, and we're going—"

"I know, baby," he said. "I heard it all. And you can't take a romantic opportunity like this and blow it with an outfit that makes you look like one of the guys."

She didn't like the fact that he wanted her to look sexy for another man, and struggling not to look hurt, she slipped the blouse off. "All right. What do you suggest?"

He went to her closet, shuffled through some of her blouses and found a soft knit blouse that clung to her in all the right places. "This is my favorite," he said. "Remember when you wore it on the hayride we chaperoned?"

"Yeah," she whispered. "We were almost the ones who needed chaperoning."

His eyes looked pained as he nodded at the memory. "He'll like it, too."

Gently, she took the blouse out of his hands and hung it up. "It's old, Jason. Besides, it's a little too low-cut."

He swallowed and turned back to her clothes. "Then how about this one?" He pulled out a Victorian-looking ivory blouse with lace that covered her breasts and rose to the high collar at her throat. "It's sexy on you. Real sexy. I couldn't keep my mind on anything else when you wore it with your hair up and those little schoolmarm glasses of yours...."

"No, Jason," she whispered, taking the blouse and hanging it back up. "I don't think I can be sexy with Danny. Besides, it's too formal. What about this?"

She pulled out an aqua polo shirt and a pair of white jeans, and Jason considered them. "Yeah," he said finally, his voice soft. "This blouse looks great with your coloring. And you have those sexy long earrings that go with it, don't you?" His voice was almost a whisper when he added, "And I happen to know that Danny really likes you in these jeans."

"Oh, he does, does he?"

He nodded. "I've caught a glance a few times when you were walking away. 'Course, he probably beat himself up the rest of the night about it."

"You're crazy," she said, frustratedly taking the outfit and leaving the closet. "And I think this idea you have about the two of us is wishful thinking. He doesn't think of me that way at all."

Jason leaned against the casing to the closet door. "Then why didn't he waste any time coming over here after work today? How come you're the one he wants to watch the meteor shower with tonight instead of one of his regular dates?"

"We're good friends, Jason. That's all we've ever been."

"There's no natural law that says good friends can't wind up lovers."

"Well, there probably is one about a deceased husband fixing his wife up with one."

Jason looked at his feet, knowing that she was right. Finally, pushing off from the door, he went to the bed, lay down and crossed his hands behind his head again. "Just get ready."

Sabrina looked at him. "I thought you said this was a bad idea. Your watching me dress and all."

"I can handle it. I always used to watch you dress, didn't I?"

She smiled sadly. "Well, yes, but you also used to take advantage of it. I'd put the bra on, you'd take it off. I'd pull the pants up..."

"I'd pull them off." His face sobered, and his eyes reflected a misty longing. "Don't worry, Bree. I can't do that anymore."

Her eyes filled unexpectedly. "I wasn't worried, Jase."

Slowly, she bent over to step into the jeans, revealing too much of what her bra covered. When her eyes met his, they were luminescent, and she saw the heat flushing his face. She straightened.

His Adam's apple bobbed. "Maybe I should leave before I get myself into trouble."

"No," she said quickly. "Please don't go. I'll get dressed."

He lay motionless, those hands still clasped behind his head and that poignant, profound look on his face as she pulled on her jeans and zipped them.

Again their eyes collided and she whispered, "You're sure they won't revoke your privileges for lusting?"

He drew in a deep breath. "I told you. It's no sin to lust after your wife." Then with a slow, maddening grin, he said, "But just in case, you'd better go ahead and put the blouse on."

She did as she was told, aware every moment of his eyes following each move she made, his mind registering every inch of her, his spirit dueling with the humanity that still lived within him.

Opening a drawer, she pulled out an aqua, white and red scarf, draped it around her neck and tied it loosely. Turning to him, she struck a pose, waiting for his approval.

"The earrings," he said in a gravelly voice.

She went to her jewelry box and got out the earrings that matched the blouse, then put them on. "Now."

For a long moment he was quiet, and finally he swallowed again. "You're an exceptionally beautiful woman," he said in a husky voice.

Her smile faded as that old familiar pain rose in her heart. "Too bad you can't do anything about it."

"Don't tempt me," he whispered seriously.

Holding his gaze, she tucked her shirt in. "You know," she said, "you acted like you wanted me to get psyched up about going out with Danny, but then you lie on my bed, looking like the answer to a prayer and watching me with those sensuous, smoky eyes, and I can't think about anything except the way we used to—"

"Don't," he whispered, his eyes misty as he gazed at her. "Don't think about what we used to do. Think about what's to come. Danny's waiting."

She stood looking at him for a moment longer, then said, "Jason..."

"Make a move tonight, baby," he whispered somberly. "Tell him I want you together. Do something to get this thing rolling."

She sighed. "I'm not ready for this."

"Yes, you are," he said. "You're more ready than you'll admit even to yourself. And Danny's ready. And when he gets a load of you in a few minutes, he's going to be so ready he won't be able to think about anything else." He got up from the bed, hooked a finger for her to come closer, and when she walked toward him, he looked into her face.

His breath smelled the way it always had, minty and fresh, as if he'd just brushed his teeth, and that hint of cologne wafted around her. Strange, that she could feel his warmth when he was only a ghost. Or an angel. Or whatever it was they called him.

"Do you feel as beautiful as you look?" he whispered.

She took in a deep breath. "You make me feel beautiful. You always did."

"You don't need me for that," he whispered. "You're gorgeous, and you need to know it. Go down there knowing that, okay?"

Her eyes misted as she nodded. "Okay."

"And enjoy the meteor shower. I'll be watching from the other side." Their eyes locked for the longest moment, and finally she raised her hand as if to touch his lips. But before her eyes, he faded away.

And she was left with only the scent of his having been, and the heat of his having loved, and the blush of his having admired her.

And lifting her chin and smiling with a little hint of anticipation, she started down the stairs.

SABRINA COULDN'T REMEMBER the last time she had laughed so much over dinner. The relief and relaxation she felt was like being miraculously healed of a painful disease. She could finally breathe, and as they left and headed out for a quiet country field from which they would watch the meteor shower without the lights of the city to dim the view, she realized she hadn't thought of Steven in hours. Jason, however, seemed to be right there with them, joining in the bantering, the laughter, the silliness—just like old times.

"A friend of mine was sitting out on her porch one night, and a meteor shot through the sky and landed on the street in front of her house."

"It did not," Sabrina said.

"Yes, it did," Danny argued. "I swear. It exploded like a fireball and rolled down the street."

"Give me a break. Did she tell you that?"

"She didn't have to tell me. I was there."

"Oh, right. You forgot to mention that at the beginning of the story."

"So sue me. And then we saw this saucerlike object with flashing lights."

She smiled and threw in, "And it swooped down and ate the fireball?"

With an amused glint in his eye, he said, "Of course not. The ball bounced up and kind of spiked itself into the saucer."

"And the lights started flashing two points?"

Danny feigned a surprised look. "How did you know? Have I told you this story?"

She covered her face with her hand and gave in to her laughter, and after Danny's laughter had died, he said, "She really did see a meteor, though. While I was talking to her on the phone."

"You're a nut, you know it?"

"So I've been told," he said. "What do you think? Does this look like a good spot?"

"Yeah," she said. "It's fine."

They pulled off the road and got out of the truck. Danny opened the tailgate and grabbed a blanket. After shaking it out, he laid it down.

"What's that for?" she asked, suddenly feeling a little uncomfortable.

"For us to lie on. We'll break our necks if we have to keep looking up. It's better lying down."

She could just hear her husband, wherever he was, snickering at the double entendre that she knew Danny hadn't meant. But Sabrina didn't find it funny at all.

THE TRUTH WAS, Jason didn't find it funny, either. As he stood outside the truck, watching Danny prepare a comfortable pallet for her in the bed of his truck, he was stricken with that confusing mixture of relief and despair.

When he'd finished making the pallet, Danny opened the ice chest he'd brought and tossed her a soda. "Now," he said. "Everything we could possibly need." Gesturing toward the makeshift bed, he said, "After you."

Sabrina climbed onto the truck bed, popped the top of her drink and looked at the stars. Almost the moment she looked up, a star shot across the sky in a majestic arc. "Look! Did you see that?"

"Yeah," Danny said in a reverent voice, lying down and lacing his fingers behind his head. "I told you it would be worth the drive."

She lay down beside him, and they lay quietly for several moments, as if the irreverence of speech might allay any possibility of another star shooting by. It was a comfortable silence, one that only Jason found uncomfortable. He was supposed to be happy, watching her grow closer to Danny. That was what his mission was all about. It was the right thing. He loved them both, and they already loved each other. It was only natural that they'd wind up together.

But he couldn't escape the plaguing thought that the closer she grew to Danny, the farther away from him she'd be.

Another star launched in a smaller arc, then disappeared as quickly as it had appeared. "Wasn't that glorious?" Danny asked on a breath of wonder.

"Beautiful," she whispered.

"It's funny, isn't it, that man can come up with all sorts of gadgets and gizmos, all kind of entertainments, all kinds of art, but we've never, in all the years this planet's been alive, been able to make anything even remotely as beautiful as that."

For the first time since they had lain down, Sabrina took her eyes off the sky and looked at the man next to her. "It's amazing, isn't it?" she asked. "And what's even stranger is that those stars are up there every night, but I rarely look at them. It's almost like I'm seeing them for the first time tonight."

He sighed. "I look at them a lot," he said. "At night, I spend a lot of time out on my deck, with my feet propped on the rail and my chair tipped back, just looking at the stars and wondering..."

"Wondering what?"

"Wondering how Jason's doing. If he's somewhere out there."

Jason smiled. *If only you knew,* he thought.

Instead of making her uncomfortable, Danny's words only seemed to draw them closer together.

"He's out there," she said with complete assurance. "And he's giving heaven a terrible time. He never was one who liked playing by the rules."

Not realizing that she spoke from absolute knowledge, Danny laughed softly. "Yeah, I can see Jason trying to shake the place up and institute a few changes. Of course, I've always thought that heaven was what life could have been like if it could be anything you wanted it to be. If that's the case, there wouldn't be much to change."

"You'd be surprised," she said softly. "I think if Jason didn't want to change heaven, he might want to change what's happening here."

Danny abandoned the stars and turned his head to look at her. "What do you mean?"

"I don't know," she said. "Maybe he would try to redirect my life. Try to keep me from screwing up."

"That sounds like Jason," Danny said. "If it could be done, I know he would do it." He considered that for a moment, then turned his head to her. His eyes were blue and glistening in the starlight as he gazed at her. "Is that why you broke up with Steven?"

"Sort of," she whispered. "I don't think Jason would have approved of him. I think he had his eye set on someone else for me."

"Yeah?" Danny asked. "Who?"

It was the perfect moment to break the ice, Jason thought, to tell Danny what Jason had told her. There would probably never be a better moment.

But Sabrina couldn't form the words.

"I don't know," she whispered. "This all must sound crazy to you."

"Not a bit," Danny said with certainty. "But I don't know if I agree with you. I can't see Jason wanting you with anyone else. He was always the jealous type." He laughed softly. "His jealousy almost ruined our friendship, you know. I'll never forget the time I told him how beautiful you are, and what a lucky man he was. He completely overreacted and misunderstood."

She smiled. "That was such a sweet thing to say, Danny."

He looked self-conscious, as if he wished he hadn't brought it up. "Yeah, well, he didn't think so. He went ballistic and said some things that made me want to deck him. The next day he apologized, though. He knew I'd never go after his girl."

"But it's different now," she whispered. "I think he'd put my happiness first. I think he'd really want to see me happy."

"Maybe," Danny said, turning back to the stars. "I don't think he'd want you to be alone for the rest of your life."

"He wouldn't want you alone for the rest of your life, either," she said.

"It's not the same thing. I'll marry someday, when the right person comes along. There's no hurry." He reached for her hand, lifted it, fondling her fingers as naturally as if he did it all the time.

Jason watched the play of their hands together, the sensuous way they touched, and his fingertips ached for the feel of her skin, the special texture that sent his libido into orbit. His heart ached at the easy way Danny touched her, the way the moonlight played on her eyes as she looked at him, the way they smiled so softly....

But this was a good thing, that other part of him told him. This was what he wanted. Somehow, he'd have to separate his human yearnings from his heavenly mission. Sabrina couldn't be his anymore. He wanted her to be Danny's now. And this was the moment, the one that would be the turning point in Sabrina's life, the one that would send her on the road to happiness.

Only then could Jason be happy.

Danny's fingers closed around her hand. "Besides," he said, "what do I need with a wife when

I've got you? It's great having a pal you can depend on."

Sabrina knew she had dropped the ball, but somehow she couldn't pick it up. Danny wasn't going to think of her that way, and that was all there was to it.

"Look, there's another one."

Her eyes darted to the sky just as the meteor played itself out, and Danny let go of her hand. She sat up and reached for her drink.

That was when she saw Jason, leaning on the rim of the truck bed, looking at her with consternation. "You blew it, Bree. A perfect opportunity to tell him what I've told you. He would have believed you, too."

She glanced at Danny, as if he would see Jason's ghost, as well, but he was still watching the stars.

"Don't worry, he can't see me," Jason said. "And by the way, I didn't overreact *that* much. He really did have a crush on you. Still does, for Pete's sake."

She mouthed for him to go away, but he only laughed.

"I'll go away when you say something to him. Something a little more definitive. Tell the guy I won't smother him in his sleep if he falls for you. Tell the idiot I love him."

Her face suggested that she didn't see the hurry, and finally he said, "I can't keep coming back indefinitely, baby. Do you want me to go through eternity wondering what happened to you? They'll pull the plug on these visits before you know it. Make a move, okay? Now's the time."

Again, she glanced at Danny, and he frowned at the turmoil he saw on her face. "Something wrong?"

She turned to Jason, but he had disappeared. Her hands were shaking as she lay down and covered her face.

"Sabrina?" Danny pressed, rising up on one elbow. "You look pale. Are you okay?"

"Yeah," she said. "I'm fine." But she wasn't fine. She actually felt a little sick, but she realized that Jason wouldn't give her any peace for the rest of the night until she did what he said. Besides, she doubted if she could sleep tonight wondering what might have happened.

"Do you want to go home?" Danny offered.

She shook her head. "No. But...I think it's time I told you something really weird. And you may not believe me."

"I'll believe anything you tell me," he said. "What is it?"

"No," she said, starting to smile. "It's even weirder than your meteor story. Only this one's true."

"Wow," he said, propping his head on his hand and grinning. "I can't wait."

She glanced to where Jason had stood before, but he was still gone. "It's about Jason."

Danny frowned. "Yeah?"

"Well ... I sort of ... I've been seeing him. Talking to him."

Danny didn't draw in a sharp, disbelieving breath, but rather looked at her with soft eyes. "I see him sometimes, too."

"You do?"

"Yeah," he said. "I'll see a guy that looks like him from behind or something, and my heart'll jump, and for a split second I'll think it's him—"

"No," she said, stopping him. "Not that way. That's not what I mean."

He sat up and gazed intently at her. "What then?"

"Oh, Danny," she said, covering her face again. "Please don't think I'm crazy."

"I know you're crazy," he said with a slight grin. "We're all crazy."

She swallowed. "Yeah, but this is the craziest thing yet. You see, Jason's been appearing to me. In the flesh. He says they let him come back from heaven to keep me from marrying Steven."

"Wait a minute," Danny said, frowning and trying hard to follow her. "You're telling me that you've been seeing his ghost? That he's actually *talking* to you?"

"Yes," she said. "Only ... he's more like an angel. I mean, I can't see through him or anything, and it doesn't get all cold— Oh, this sounds so ludicrous."

"You told me this before, didn't you?"

She tried to remember, but couldn't. "When?"

"At the engagement party. You said that you felt his presence, like he was standing in front of you. Had you seen him then?"

"Yes," she said, "but I didn't want to come right out and say it, because I thought maybe I *was* going crazy. But now I know I'm not. It's really him, and I see him all the time. He was just here, a minute ago."

"Here?" Danny looked around. "Where?"

"Right there, standing by the truck. He was talking to me. He wanted me to tell you—" She hesitated, knowing that all this was too much for Danny to take in. He'd have to deal with Jason's appearances first before he could deal with the bomb she had to drop on him. "He wanted me to tell you that I saw him. He thought you'd believe me."

"Wow." He moved to the edge of the truck and looked around in the night. "And you say he was here a minute ago? Why didn't I see him?"

"He can only appear to me. You see, he had to get permission from some committee in heaven, and apparently it's real unusual for them to let somebody come back like this."

"I should think so."

The serious tone of his voice suddenly struck Sabrina as funny, and she realized that Danny didn't really buy the whole thing. He was just trying not to offend her by doubting. She started to laugh softly, at first, but then louder, until she lay down and covered her face. Danny began to laugh, too.

"What's so funny?" he asked through his laughter.

"You," she said. "You're trying so hard not to call me nuts. You're probably trying to figure out the best way to have me committed without my freaking out entirely."

"No, I'm not," he said. "I believe you think you've seen Jason."

"I don't think it, Danny. It's true." Her laughter faded, though she knew it could return any moment. "Seriously. I'm not making this up, and I'm not crazy."

"Okay." He cleared his throat and tried not to smile. "All right, then. If you saw him, I believe you."

Knowing he still really didn't, she tried to think of some things to convince him. "He told me that you liked these jeans on me."

Danny's smile faded. "He did?"

"Yes, he did. Said he'd caught a glance or something."

"You didn't have those when he was alive. You just bought them a couple of months ago."

The fact that he knew when she'd bought them told her that something about them had registered in his mind. "Well, I know, but I guess sometimes he's around when we're together. Like tonight. He just can't appear to you."

In the darkness, she saw color shade across Danny's face and knew the exact second when he went from doubt to near belief. "Terrific. He's watching everything I do?"

"No, of course not. Not everything. He does have some decorum, you know. And he's not here all the time."

"So I looked at you once or twice." A slow grin crept across his mouth. "Or a dozen times. You're a good-looking lady. I'm not blind, you know. Anybody would."

She laughed. "It's okay, Danny. He's not mad. It was just a point of information."

"All right, what else did he tell you?"

She knew that he still didn't entirely believe, so she sought her memory for other things. "Well, he told me that Steven was after my money. It kind of turned out to be true."

"No, about me. What else did he tell you about me?"

She knew it was the time to tell him the rest—that Jason wanted the two of them together—but something still stopped her. She just wasn't ready. And she knew Danny wasn't.

"Well... He told me that you... that you had a picture of me... in your bedroom."

He looked like he'd just been speared in the heart, and he dropped down and stared at the sky. "I don't believe this."

"I know it's hard, but—"

"Why is he telling you this stuff? Is he mad at me, or what?"

It was then that she knew he had no doubts at all, that he absolutely believed every word of this ridiculous story that happened to be true and that he was smarting over what she'd said.

"No, he isn't mad. He loves you."

"Yeah, right. Then why is he trying to humiliate me like this? I'd kill him if he weren't already dead."

She giggled. "You'd have to beat me to it. He isn't trying to humiliate you, Danny. He just told me so... Well, you know..." She still couldn't make herself say it, so finally she changed her story. "So I'd have something to tell you to make you believe, I guess. And it worked, didn't it?"

"Yeah, it worked," Danny said. "And tell him I said it was very funny. And by the way, I have pictures of a lot of people in my bedroom. My parents included."

"You don't owe me an explanation."

"I even have a picture of Jason stuck in my mirror. Did he tell you that?"

"Danny, he wasn't trying to make anything of it. It was just something—"

He started to laugh then, and she realized he was letting go of his brief little flare-up of anger. "That guy beats everything," he said. "Tell him I said that."

"He misses you, too."

Danny smiled. "Imagine him leaving heaven to straighten you out. That's Jason, all right."

"Yeah," she whispered as another meteor shot across the sky. But this time she didn't squeal or tell Danny to look. This time it didn't seem so far-fetched that the heavens could behave that way. She only wondered if Jason had seen it, too. "I think Jason plans to straighten us both out."

But she didn't say how, because despite Jason's urgings, she knew it wasn't time. Maybe later she'd tell Danny that their destinies were intertwined. But now she'd just enjoy his company while the heavens entertained them.

Chapter Six

When Sabrina came in that night, she saw Jason lying on her bed with his feet crossed and his hands behind his head. He wasn't grinning that smug, maddening little grin with which he usually met her. Instead, his countenance was sober.

"That was pretty good, what you did tonight," he said.

She dropped her purse on her dresser and looked at him. "You're not mad that I didn't ask him to marry me?"

She saw the hint of his smile. "You won't have to. He'll ask you. I just wanted you to tell him that he's supposed to."

Smiling, she sat down next to him and pulled her feet up on the bed, hugging her knees. "Well, I decided it was best not to hit him with everything all at once. He's a little put out with you, you know."

His grin blossomed across his face. "I know he is. But if you noticed, he didn't deny any of it. He'll get over it as soon as he realizes what I left him."

"What?" she asked.

His smile faded again, and his eyes softened. "My wife," he whispered. "The most precious gift I could give."

"I don't much like being thought of as a gift, Jason."

"I know, baby," he said. "And it's not like you're a possession. But you are precious."

Her heart swelled, the way it never had in Steven's presence and the way it hadn't yet in Danny's. She took in a deep breath, longing to lie down next to him, lay her head on his chest, run her fingers through the hair there. Before he died, some of his chest hair had begun to turn gray. She wondered now if it had gone grayer, or if it was dark again, as it had been in his youth. It didn't matter to her what color it was. She longed to feel it curling under her fingers, his heart beating against her face, to feel him holding her so tightly that she never had a doubt in the world that she was safe. She longed to feel his body responding to just the sight of her, longed to feel their legs entertwining, tangling, as he rolled her over....

"What's wrong?" Jason asked, breaking the quiet.

She blinked the tears threatening to assault her, and as she looked at him, she knew he'd been thinking all the same thoughts. He knew what was wrong.

"Why can't I touch you?" she whispered.

"They have all sorts of reasons," he said, his voice a sensual caress. "They feel it would be counterproductive, that it would only end in more grief for both of us, that you'd be even less inclined to let go, that *I'd* never fully surrender to heaven. But the biggest reason of all is the purity thing. They know it would be too tempting. That maybe we wouldn't stop at touching."

"Maybe we wouldn't," she whispered, her eyes smoky at the very thought. "But what would be the harm? You held me once, that first time you came back. Remember, Jason? And they still let you come back."

"Not without some very stern warnings. I don't think I'll get another chance."

They stayed quiet, sharing their personal anguish, reveling in memories of touches and caresses, memories that couldn't be repeated. "You know what I wish?" he asked finally.

"What?"

"I wish that I had savored those moments when I could touch you. I wish I had spent more time holding you, kissing you, breathing you...."

A tear dropped to her cheek, and she nodded. "I wish the same thing. I sometimes have this fantasy...." She swallowed and wiped the tears gathering under her eyes. "A fantasy that everybody in the world is allowed one chance to turn back time and erase a tragedy or a mistake. That one time in everybody's life, they get a second chance. And I fantasize that I can turn back time and wake up one day before you were ever in that accident and that I'd keep you from getting in that car that day and that we'd have a whole lifetime together."

He sat up, slowly moving closer, and she saw the tears in his eyes, the anguish, the lost wishes and the unanswered prayers. She hugged herself tighter as he touched the scarf around her neck and pulled her closer to him.

She shivered with restraint as she tried not to melt into him, against him, tried not to slide her hands around his neck, for if she did, she knew that he would be taken away. Maybe for the last time.

"Do you think . . . that maybe this could be some kind of hell for us?" she asked on a wavering whisper. "That maybe you weren't supposed to go to heaven, and this is the cruel way that you're suffering out your eternity?"

"No, baby," he said. "This wasn't meant to be a cruel joke. It was my time, and they didn't mean to torment me by letting me come back. They were trying to make me happy."

"But it is hell, Jason."

"You don't belong in hell, baby. That's why I want you to let me go. That's why I want you to find happiness again."

She breathed in a deep sigh and whispered, "I'm trying."

She shivered again, and slowly he began to unbutton his shirt, one button at a time, peeling back the cloth to reveal the chest she had missed so much, with all the masculine, unaged brown curls that covered it, and the capability there, and the strength. He pulled the shirt off his broad, athletic shoulders and slipped his arms out. Then he put it over her shoulders, careful not to touch her, and pulled the big shirt around her.

Immediately, she felt his warmth like an embrace, and closed her eyes, feeling the cloth tighten around her as he pulled it as close to him as he could without touching her.

Every sense came alive in her, every fiber of feeling, and she agonized to touch him, run her lips along the silky skin at his throat, hug him with her legs and her arms until they melded into one being....

She opened her eyes and looked at the agony on his face and took the scarf off her neck. Slowly, she put it around his neck, careful not to touch him, and pulled the ends until his face was only millimeters from hers. He closed his eyes and imagined it was her arms around his neck, that she was stroking her thumb through his hair, that her head was arched back as she gazed at him as if he were the only person in the world.

"You always made me feel so special," he whispered. "Do you know what a happy man you made me every day when I came home from work and you greeted me at the door with that radiant smile?"

Another tear dropped, but neither of them wiped it away.

"That was such a heaven in itself," he whispered, "and they've promised that when I let you go, I'll have that a thousandfold. But I guess I have trouble trusting that. My faith is just too weak."

"It will be, Jase. They couldn't call it heaven if it wasn't way better than anything here."

"It's hard to believe that anything's better than your smile."

They sat that way for a short eternity, Jason holding the edges of the shirt that embraced her, Sabrina clutching the ends of the scarf that circled him.

"Will I ever stop loving you?" she whispered.

He sucked in a tormented breath. "I hope not," he whispered. "But someday you'll love again. Someday you'll love Danny."

But it was hard to believe that.

Slowly, he faded out of her sight. The shirt he'd had around her faded, as well, and her scarf fell limp on the bed in front of her. She felt cold and unbearably alone.

"WE'VE GOT a surprise for you." Pete's grin was mysterious, and as Jason came into the room where he'd sat before the committee so many times before, Pete winked at Mo and Dave. "Come in, Jason."

Jason hoped this wasn't some kind of trick, where they pretended to be happy with him only to reprimand him for spending too much time with Sabrina. "What surprise?"

Mo stood up, his Bermuda shorts wrinkled from where he'd been sitting, and he pulled a wrapped box from under the table.

"A present?" Jason asked. "What's the occasion?"

"No occasion," Dave said. "We just thought this was something you might like. Go ahead, open it."

Curious, Jason pulled the tape up from the edges, careful not to tear the paper.

"Come on, Jase," Pete said. "Tear into it. This is heaven. It's not like we can't get more."

"Oh, yeah." Jason tore into the package and opened the box. Slowly, he pulled out the contents. "A baseball uniform?" he asked, frowning.

"That's right," Pete said. "You're playing third base, and we managed to get you on Babe Ruth's team. Who else is on that team, Mo?"

"Don Drysdale, Roberto Clemente. Ty Cobb and Lou Gehrig are on the team you're playing tonight."

"You're kidding," Jason said. "I love those guys! Man, I saw almost every game Roberto ever played. And Lou Gehrig! Oh, man, this is great!"

Pete, Mo and Dave laughed, enjoying his enthusiasm. "We should warn you. All our teams are good. It'll take a lot of practice, but we've been assured that your talent is at its peak right now."

He laughed at the thought of playing beside Babe Ruth, and shook out the uniform. "What talent? I never really had any talent. I haven't even played on a team since high school."

"Well, you have it now," Pete said. "We don't guarantee a homer on every at-bat. That wouldn't be any fun. But you've got what it takes, Jason. You just have to hone it."

Mo added, "It'll take a lot of practice."

Suddenly, Jason realized what they were up to, and his smile crashed as he dropped the uniform into the box. "Oh, I get it. You're trying to divert my attention. Keep me busy so I won't want to keep going back."

Dave shot an I-told-you-so look to the others. "Your job is done there, Jason. There's no reason to hang around."

"But she isn't with Danny yet. I have to make sure they get together."

"How do you think anyone ever manages without your guidance?" Mo asked.

Jason recognized the sarcasm and didn't respond.

"Sabrina will be taken care of," Pete said softly. "There's a divine plan for her, and she won't be abandoned. He never abandons anyone."

"I know He doesn't," Jason said, dropping into a chair and burying his face in his hands. "I'm not doubting that. I guess it's just for my own peace of mind." He looked at the uniform again, and shrugged. "Don't you realize that I want to get along here? I'd love to play third base on Babe Ruth's team. I'd love to fall in love with one of the pretty little angels I've seen. I'd love to close the door on the past and dive into eternity. But I'm having a hard time."

"Yes, well, it doesn't help when you watch her undress and play little romantic pantomime love scenes with her," Dave said.

"Hey, I didn't touch her!" Jason defended. "You can't say I touched her."

"You did everything *but* touch her," Mo said. "Jason, we're not trying to be hard-nosed. We just think it's time that you gave it up."

"I will," he assured them. "I promise. Just give me a little more time. It won't take much. I have to see that she's all right. I have to know that she can be happy again."

Pete sighed and slumped back in his chair. "You can keep going, Jason, for a little while longer, if you'll join the team now. Today. We want you practicing and playing, and in your spare time you can check on Sabrina. But it can't be your main focus anymore. We won't have it."

"Okay," he said quickly. "It's a deal. I'll play third base. Are you guys coming to the games?"

"Are you kidding?" Mo asked. "We have season tickets."

"I've got dibs on the first home-run ball you hit," Dave said. "I collect them, you know."

Jason nodded. "You got it. I guess it's good that you have a whole eternity to wait for one." He stood up and took the box and glanced at his watch. Sabrina was probably just waking up right about now, making her coffee and getting ready to go to work. If he hurried, he might have time to—

"Practice starts in ten minutes, and they're expecting you today. There's a big game tonight," Pete said. "You'd better go on over."

Jason's heart sank. "Yeah, okay. I will. Thanks, guys."

"Enjoy it, Jason," Pete added as he left the room. "We really want you to enjoy it."

FELONY AND MISDEMEANOR, the two cats that shared a house with Danny, stretched and climbed on his chest as he lay on his bed, unwinding after a day in court. It had been a tedious case that he had finally won, but throughout it all, he hadn't been able to keep his mind off Sabrina.

"I should be shot, shouldn't I, Misdee?" he asked the older of the two cats as he stroked her silver and white coat. "Just thinking about her, I'm betraying my best friend." The cat yawned, and the other one nuzzled up to his neck and licked his chin. "Yeah, I know, Felony. I do deserve a little break in the love department. Heaven knows I've looked long enough for Ms. Right."

He scooped both cats off him and got up, turned on his television and thought about food. He had to eat, yet he hated to cook, and the thought of eating out alone tonight didn't appeal to him at all. He went to the cabinet, hoping for a three-course dinner to appear miraculously, but all he had there was a bag of stale potato chips, a jar of bacon bits and a can of bay leaves. Abandoning that in favor of the refrigerator, he perused the contents as the cats stood beside him. He looked forlornly at the month-old milk, the half bottle of Coke and the eggs he had boiled weeks ago so they wouldn't go bad.... But he suspected they had, anyway.

"Guess that seals it," he told the cats, closing the refrigerator door. "I have to eat out. And if I call and invite her along, it doesn't mean a thing, does it? I mean, if I had a sister, I'd invite her, wouldn't I? There's no difference in that and taking your best friend's wife out to dinner."

Satisfied that he had proper justification for doing such a thing, he went to the phone and dialed Sabrina's number.

"Hello?"

"Hey, there," Danny said, smiling at the sound of her voice. He could hear her smile, too, as she answered.

"What's up, Danny? How was court today?"

"Great. Won the case. Now I deserve to celebrate."

"I should say so."

"Wanna go get something to eat?"

"Sure," she said. "The only thing I have in the house is rice. I was going to cook it tonight, but what the heck?"

He chuckled and glanced at the clock. "Forty-five minutes all right?"

"Sure," she said. "Where are we going?"

"Someplace nice. Wear your dancing shoes."

There was a slight pause, then, "Okay. I'll be ready."

Her voice had changed, he realized as he hung up. The moment he had suggested their dancing, she'd gotten quieter. It was a subtle difference, but he had caught it. He turned around, hands on his hips, and caught Misdemeanor staring at him.

"I know, Misdee," he said. "If I keep this up, I'll ruin a friendship. Make her afraid to be around me at all. Not to mention the fact that Jason will start haunting me, sliming my house, rattling chains, taking revenge in subtle little ways." He shook his head, fighting the conflicting feelings at war in his mind. "Don't worry, I'll cool it. And I'll get over it, too. I can beat this thing."

But after he'd gotten ready, dressed in his best suit and worn his sexiest cologne, after he'd polished his shoes and shaved for the second time that day, he realized that it wasn't going to be all that easy to beat, after all. But he could keep it in check. No one would ever have to know.

IT WAS THE FIRST home run Jason had hit since Little League, but that time it had been against Squirrel McKinley rather than Christy Mathewson. The crowd in the stands came to their feet, and he could hear their delirious squeals and their Arsenio whoops as he tore around the bases.

The team waited for him at the plate, cheering him as if he were the star player. Roberto, Babe, Don—all whooped and hollered and patted him on the back. Behind the dugout, Pete stood, flashing him a thumbs-up. Mo was leaning into the fence, yelling and hollering like any of the other fans, and he could hear Dave's voice as it thundered out over the diamond, "Way to go, Jase, my boy. Way to go!"

The feeling was pure, hundred-proof ecstasy, and as he went to the dugout, he thought how proud Sabrina would have been of him, if she could only have seen it. He couldn't wait to tell her.

"Hey, Jason." Jason turned around and saw Dave standing with a woman with long, curling red hair and a smile that rivaled Julia Roberts's. "I want you to meet Beth. She's a new fan of yours."

"Hi, Beth," he said, tipping his cap.

"That was great hitting," she said. "For a lawyer."

He frowned. "You don't like lawyers?"

"I am one," she said. "Or I was. What was your specialty?"

"Contract law," he said. "But my partner and I did some litigation and a lot of general work, too."

"My practice was general, too. 'Course, not anymore. They don't need lawyers here, do they?"

"That's okay," he said. "We don't need the money here."

She laughed, gave a short salute. "Well, it was great meeting you. Would you by any chance like to get a cup of coffee after the game?"

His smile faded, and he glanced at Dave. "Uh, no. I'm afraid I have a prior commitment."

"That's okay," she said. "I'll see you later."

As she walked off, he gave Dave an accusing look. Dave only returned it.

"Man, you must be crazy to pass up a date with her."

"I wish you and your buddies would stop trying to fix me up, Dave. I don't need it."

"Hey, I wasn't trying to fix anybody up. She asked me to introduce her."

Jason looked into the stands where she had sat down. She was pretty. No doubt about that. But no matter how pretty she was, he doubted she could ever make him feel the way Sabrina did.

He looked at his watch and wondered if she was back from her date with Danny. The last time he'd checked on her, Danny was just picking her up. He hadn't appeared to her. There hadn't been time before he'd been due at practice.

"You're not supposed to wear a watch in heaven," Dave said, his voice edged with disgust.

"I'm keeping up with earth time," he said. "It keeps me straight."

Dave sighed. "Look, Beth isn't going anywhere. Why don't you two get together tomorrow? You probably have a lot in common. There aren't that many lawyers here, you know."

Jason grinned at the stab at his profession. "I'll think about it."

"Please do," Dave said. "And don't miss any practices. They're counting on you now."

"I won't." He turned to the game as Dave walked off, his regal stride commanding more attention than that of Babe Ruth on the field.

And as Roberto hit another home run, Jason glanced at his watch and tried to imagine where Danny and Sabrina were now.

SABRINA COVERED HER MOUTH with both hands to suppress her laughter over the imitation Danny did of the defendant in the case of the irate neighbor versus the family he referred to as the Hillbilly Hoarders. It seemed that the hillbillies considered the mound of junk in their front yard to be a work of art, but the neighbors didn't appreciate it.

"Not all art is purty," Danny said, smacking his lips in his impression of the toothless patriarch of the household. "And don't all of it smell good."

The waiter approached the table, offering to refill their glasses, but Sabrina could only shake her head in response.

When she finally caught her breath, she asked, "You won the case?"

"It wasn't easy," he said. "He made a good case for the fact that rodents are a natural part of the outdoors, and it took a lot of evidence to prove that his masterpiece was attracting them. But I managed to."

"So what did he wind up doing with the mound of junk?"

At this point, Danny almost lost himself to his own laughter. "He tried to sell it to a museum. No one would buy it. I believe it's now resting in a landfill somewhere, although I've heard he's working on building another one in his living room."

Again, she gave in to her amusement and covered her mouth, when suddenly Danny's smile collapsed. Someone was standing behind her.

"I'm glad to see you're having such a good time with my fiancée."

Sabrina jerked around. "Steven!"

He stood over their table, his hands in his pockets and that tiny vein in his temple throbbing with lethal urgency.

Danny stood up slowly. "She's not your fiancée, anymore."

Steven bent to Sabrina and braced himself on the arms of her chair. His breath smelled of Scotch, and his bloodshot eyes told her he'd been drinking for some time. "Darling, we need to talk. Everything that happened a few days ago, it was a mistake. We were angry and we said things we didn't mean."

"Steven, we really don't have anything to talk about." She tried to keep her voice calm, discreet, so there wouldn't be a scene. "We made the right decision."

"No, *we* didn't," he said. "You made this decision. I still want to marry you. We can work this out, if only we can go somewhere private and talk." He grabbed her arm and tried to pull her to her feet. "Come on, honey. Come with me."

Danny grabbed his arm. "She's with me tonight," he said through his teeth. "Now get the hell out of here."

Steven stood straighter and wrenched his wrist from Danny's grip. "I'm not going anywhere without her."

"She's not going anywhere with you," Danny bit out. "And if you don't leave in the next five seconds, I'll take you out myself."

Breathless, Sabrina stood up. "Please, Steven. Just go home."

Steven's eyes were still locked on Danny's. "I'm getting sick and tired of your interference, man.

After we're married, your relationship is going to change."

"There isn't going to be a wedding," Sabrina insisted. "Now, Steven, don't make a scene. Just leave."

Steven stood his ground, though he had to steady himself on the edge of her chair. "Not without you," he said.

"Don't make me embarrass us all," Danny said, "because it will when I physically throw you out of here myself. You have five seconds to disappear."

When Steven made no move to walk away, Danny grabbed his arm and jerked it behind his back. "Let's go," he said, shoving him toward the door.

Steven shook free and swung around. "What is it with you, man?" he yelled, disregarding the diners, all watching the scene with dismay. "Do you want her for yourself? Is that why she's been so confused lately? Are you trying to get into her pants while she's vulnerable? The good guy who's there to pick up the pieces?"

Sabrina screamed as Danny grabbed Steven's collar and his fist flew into the man's jaw, knocking him back and into a table of patrons behind them.

A flurry of screams followed, and the maître d' rushed forward, babbling something about their leaving as soon as possible.

Danny tossed a hundred-dollar bill on the table to cover dinner and a tip, then grabbed Sabrina's hand.

Behind them, the maître d' helped Steven to his feet. At the sight of the blood on his lip, he shouted, "Should I call an ambulance?"

"You'd better do that," Danny answered before Steven could. "Tell them to give him a sedative and lock him up, before he really gets hurt."

Sabrina let Danny pull her out the door.

Danny didn't say a word all the way home, and Sabrina wasn't sure whether he was angry at her, beating up himself or reliving the madness of what had just happened.

When they got home, she urged him to come in so she could bandage the scrape on his hand from where his fist had met Steven's jaw. Reluctantly, he followed her in, still brooding. Shrugging out of his coat, he dropped down on the couch and gave her his hand.

Carefully, she took it. "You must have hit him pretty hard. This looks bad."

He winced as she painted it with iodine, then wrapped a gauze bandage over his knuckles. "We didn't get to dance," he said quietly.

"It's okay," she said. "They wouldn't have let us stay, after that."

He dropped his head on the sofa cushions and closed his eyes. "I'm really sorry. I've never lost my head like that. The last time I was in a fight, I was in the sixth grade and some guy ran over my pet lizard with his bike."

"Wow," she said. "I ranked right up there with your lizard, huh? I'm flattered."

Despite himself, he smiled. "You should be. She was my first love."

She finished the bandage but didn't let go of his hand. "I appreciate what you did, Danny. He deserved it."

"But it was so barbaric," he said, his smile fading again. "So Neanderthal."

"Actually," she said with the hint of a grin, "I'm a little ashamed that I enjoyed it."

Again, his smile inched across his face. "Yeah?"

"Yeah," she said. "To have two men fighting over me... Isn't that every woman's secret fantasy?"

"Not yours."

She lifted her brows. "You might be surprised."

He gazed at her for a moment, a spark of challenge in his eye, and asked, "What would Jason say?"

"I think he'd be proud," she said.

He was quiet for a moment longer, and finally Sabrina felt that old awkwardness creeping on them again. Picking up the remote control, she flicked on the television. A slow Rod Stewart song was playing on VH1, and she glanced at Danny. He was still staring pensively at her. Slowly, she stood up and held her hand out for his. "Come on, Danny. We can dance here."

He looked a little uncomfortable, but he got up anyway and took her hands. When she set one at his shoulder and moved closer, he seemed to grow more tense.

Closing her eyes, Sabrina tried to think of him in terms she hadn't really before. Not as Danny her best pal, but as Danny the man, the one who'd broken so many hearts. The fit was natural, and she realized that he had a comfortable embrace. He was bigger than Steven, broader, and his arms felt better around her. And he smelled nice, some forest cologne that called up images of woodchopping.

He stopped moving, and she looked up at him. "What's wrong?"

"I don't know," he said, letting her go. "This just feels weird."

"Why?" She didn't back away from him, and he didn't move, either. Their faces were close, so close that she smelled a breath mint she hadn't seen him put in his mouth.

"Because you're . . . you're my best friend's wife. I don't want you to think I'm coming on to you." His voice was deep, rugged. "The scene in the restaurant might have been confusing, I mean with me acting like your hero, or something. But I don't want you to think . . ."

"Why don't you want me to think that?" she whispered.

"Because I don't want you to be uncomfortable around me. I don't want you making excuses to avoid me. I couldn't stand that."

"Why on earth would I do that?"

Slowly, he backed away from her and, sitting down, he rubbed his neck and let out a labored sigh. "Look, I was Jason's best friend. I loved him. I would never do anything that would betray his memory."

Sabrina sank down next to him, and staring at her hands, she said, "What if he wanted you to?"

"Betray his memory?" he asked, looking at her.

"No," she said. "What if he wanted you to... well ... us to ..."

"What?" he prompted.

She wished, for once, Danny would use his usually sharp wit to figure this out without making her say it. "I told you I'd been seeing him," she said. "Do you still believe me?"

"Yeah, I believe you," he said.

She sighed. "Well, would you believe me if I told you that the reason he's been coming was not just to make me break it off with Steven? That he also wanted to see me get involved with the right person?"

"Well, yeah. That would make sense. To me, anyway."

The words were more difficult than she imagined, yet Danny wasn't helping her at all. "Why do you think he told me about the picture in your room, or the fact that you liked my white jeans?''

Danny looked at her blankly for a moment, but then a slow grin came over his eyes. ''Because he wanted you to understand why he was going to kill me in my sleep?''

She laughed. ''No, that's not it.''

Danny took in a deep, ragged breath, and he raked a hand through his hair. His grin was still perceptive as he looked at her. ''You're gonna have to spell this out for me, Sabrina, because I'd be a fool to jump to conclusions about it.''

He *was* going to make her say it, and now she realized that she'd already said too much to turn back. ''Jason thinks that you and I would be perfect for each other. In fact, you're probably the only one on the face of the earth that he wants to see me wind up with.''

When she forced herself to look at him, he was gaping at her. ''You're kidding.''

An alarm flashed in her brain, and instantly she decided Jason was wrong about Danny's feelings, and now she looked like an idiot. It didn't matter if he was already dead, she thought. She was going to kill him anyway.

Danny leaned toward her, frowning. ''You're telling me that he wouldn't ransack heaven if he found out you and I were . . . well, that we were getting involved?''

"Not only wouldn't he ransack it," she said, "he might actually be able to enjoy it finally."

He leaned his head back on the couch, his eyes wide as he stared in front of him. "Wow. I can't believe this."

This wasn't how he was supposed to react, Sabrina told herself. If she was to believe the things Jason had told her, Danny would have admitted to an undying love of her and a burning desire to make her his own. This simple surprise, this speechlessness indicated to her that he didn't know what to do now. That he didn't know of a graceful way to tell her that it wasn't going to happen.

Yes, she was definitely going to kill him.

Finally deciding to let herself off the hook, she began changing the station as rapidly as she spoke. "I don't want you to think that I necessarily agree with him. I mean, I'm with you. I don't want to ruin our friendship, either, and it could get pretty heavy if we started thinking of each other in any other way. I mean, I don't even know if I buy the stuff about there being a plan. Jason can get pretty melodramatic sometimes, and frankly, he admitted that he can't read minds. And in heaven, his imagination is probably even more vivid than it was on earth, and it was pretty vivid then . . ."

As she spoke, Danny reached up and took the remote control out of her hands, set it on the coffee table and pushed her hair back at her neck. "Shut up," he said softly.

She hushed and set her big eyes on him, anticipating every word. "You see, the thing is..." His voice trailed off as a thumb stroked along her cheekbone, and his fingers slid through her hair, pulling her closer, "I think Jason knows what he's talking about."

She caught her breath, but before she could answer, his lips claimed hers.

It was a sweet kiss, a soft kiss, and her heart beat faster than it ever had with Steven. She closed her eyes as the kiss grew deeper, and she learned why so many women fell in love with Danny. He was good at this. Very good. And the idea of his being hers was looking better all the time.

She had trouble meeting his eyes as he broke the kiss and pulled back to look at her.

"Was that okay?" he asked her on a whisper.

She smiled. "Yes."

He swallowed and stroked her hair from her face. "I think we have an awful lot to think about," he said. "Why don't I go home, and we can both think about what this relationship would be like without the limitations of friendship. And then tomorrow, we can start all over, and see how it goes?"

Mesmerized, she nodded. "Okay."

He kissed her again, this time with more fervor and more heart-skipping intensity. And then, without a word to break the magic silence, he left her alone, hugging the pillow on the sofa and smiling, almost dazed, as the possibilities assaulted her.

DANNY WALKED TO HIS CAR with a grin on his face and hesitated before getting in. Propping his arms on the roof, he looked at the house. He couldn't believe he had kissed her. He couldn't believe she had let him. He couldn't believe how much more he wanted from her now.

But most of all, he couldn't believe his feelings had been sanctioned and that Jason was lifting the barriers that had been between Sabrina and him for so long.

He looked at the stars, sprinkling the black night in all their glory, and smiled with more serenity than he'd felt since Jason died.

"Thanks, buddy," he said.

He didn't see Jason standing on the other side of his car, leaning against a tree in his baseball uniform. But Jason saw Danny, and as his friend drove away, he gave a sad smile and whispered, "My pleasure."

But as the headlights disappeared into the night, Jason realized it was the first lie he'd told since going to heaven.

Chapter Seven

Sabrina sang softly under her breath as she got ready for bed, and for a moment Jason stood quietly behind her, watching her reflection in the mirror and trying to decide whether to approach her at all or leave her alone to think about what had happened tonight. That was the plan, after all, wasn't it? She had been pointed in the right direction, both she and Danny knew what they were supposed to do, and for all intents and purposes, his job was done.

So why was he still here?

He started to make himself leave until she opened the drawer and reached for one of his T-shirts. Something kept him from leaving as she shrugged out of her blouse, shed her bra and slipped the shirt over her head.

She looked better in a man's T-shirt than most women looked in Victoria's Secret lingerie, he thought, and for the life—or death—of him, he couldn't turn away.

She saw him in the mirror before he'd wrestled up the courage to go, and slowly she turned around.

The expression on her face was sweeter and more beautiful than he'd seen in ages, and he envied Danny for inspiring it. "Hi," she whispered.

"Hey, there," he said softly. "How's it goin'?"

"Great."

He recognized the awkwardness she felt, knowing that he knew she and Danny had kissed. He wished he knew a way to make her more comfortable with it.

"What are you wearing?" she asked softly. "A baseball uniform?"

"Yeah," he said with a laugh. "I had a game tonight. You won't believe the guys on my team. Babe Ruth, Roberto Clemente, Don Drysdale..."

"Really?" she asked, grinning. "They have baseball in heaven?"

"Sure, they do. And I happened to mention that I'd always wanted to play in the pros. Next thing I know, I'm playing third base. And if I do say so myself, I'm a dynamo on that diamond. Hit a home run tonight with the bases loaded, against Christy Mathewson."

"You're kidding." Fascinated, she came toward him with a half grin, trying to picture him in a high-stakes game with some of the best players in history. "I wish I could have seen it."

"I wish you could, too," he said with a laugh. "It was great. The ball went soaring over left field. I don't think they ever even found it. The crowd went wild."

She giggled. "I had no idea... I mean, it makes sense that there would be baseball in heaven, and that you'd be great at it. But I always imagined heaven differently."

He smiled softly. "How did you imagine it?"

"I don't know. People floating around in some kind of spiritual daze, choirs singing 'Ave Maria,' St. Peter standing at the pearly gates..."

"Well, the choir part is half-right," he said. "We have some music that you wouldn't believe. But heaven is a busy place. Everybody has something to do. And as for the pearly gates, there's no such thing. And St. Peter isn't the one who greets you. Pete happens to be on my troubleshooting committee, but he wasn't the first to greet me."

Her eyes grew wider as she took it all in. "Who was?"

"My dad," he said. "They always send someone you love."

She smiled. "Your father. Then you get to see him?"

"Sure, I do," he said. "'Course, he spends a lot of time deep-sea fishing, playing tennis and riding horses and stuff. And I've been here a lot lately."

She covered her mouth and let out a breezy laugh. "This is amazing. It sounds wonderful. What else do they have there?"

"They have everything anyone could want." His smile faded, and he added, "Everything but you."

The smile in her eyes turned melancholy, and she turned away and began straightening her dresser. "I guess you saw earlier."

He looked at his cleats. "Not all of it. The game held me up a little. But I saw the most important part."

"That's good, isn't it?" she asked, not certain. "I mean, I told Danny what you said, and he seemed to take it well."

"Take it well?" Jason breathed a laugh. "The man happens to be delirious."

She turned around then, her eyes still sad. "And what about you?"

Jason shrugged, trying to make light of it, and said, "It's what I've been working toward, isn't it?"

She tried to read the unspoken words on his face, tried to put herself in his shoes and imagine how she would feel. What if the situation was reversed, and she had tried to fix *him* up?

"Tell me something, Jason," she whispered. "Do you ever meet women in heaven?"

Laughing, he sat down on the bed. "More lately than usual. Dave and Pete have each tried to fix me up. Tonight they even found me a lady lawyer who's real impressed with baseball."

She didn't bother to ask who Dave and Pete were, for she struggled with a lump the size of her heart that was lodged in her throat. "Is she pretty?"

"Yeah," he said. "She is. But she's not you, babe. You don't have anything to worry about."

Suddenly, she felt incredibly selfish and tried to rally. "I'm not worried, Jason. I was just curious. I want you to meet somebody, fall in love again, have a companion. I want you to be happy."

"I want that, too," he said. "And when I'm finished here, maybe I'll see things differently."

"What do you mean when you're finished here?" she asked, slowly sinking down next to him on the bed.

"I mean, I can't keep coming back here forever. As soon as you're settled, my privileges will be revoked. It could happen anytime now."

"Well, then, I *won't* get settled," she said. "I'll tell Danny that I'm not ready. And you can tell them that I need you, that—"

"Don't you understand, baby, that they know?" he cut in. "There's no way to deceive them. You just have to know that I'll be around less and less now, until I stop coming completely. I won't be spying on every kiss you share with Danny, and I won't be judging you and mapping out your relationship. There has to be a point where you're on your own. It may be sooner than you think."

He saw the fear in her eyes, the despair, and he hated himself for putting it there.

"So what are you saying? That this might be your last trip? That you could literally disappear and never come back again? That I could go through the rest of my life waiting for you to reappear?''

"No," he said. "It won't be like that. I won't cut you off just like that."

"Promise me," she demanded in a desperate voice. "Promise me that you'll tell me when it's the last time. Promise me you'll say goodbye this time. If you don't, I don't know what I'll do!''

"I promise," he whispered, though he wasn't sure they would let him keep it. All he knew was that, somehow, he would. "It'll be okay, baby. I promise."

THE MORNING LIGHT filled the room with a radiance that didn't exist anywhere else in the world, and Mo adjusted his sunglasses, crossed his tanned legs at the ankle and shook his head at the other two men in the room. "I told you it wouldn't work. It didn't make him happy."

"I think it did," Pete said, "on some level. But it's got to be hard seeing your wife falling for someone else."

"Well, that's just it," Dave piped in, pulling his slingshot from his pocket and examining it. "I don't think she is happy. She's just going through the motions because it's what he wants. We've robbed her of all the spontaneity she might have had. I think we've allowed this to go just a little too far."

"All right," Pete said with a heavy sigh. "Then when he comes in this morning, tell him it's over. He can't go back."

Dave sat up straight. "Me tell him? I'm not gonna tell him." He aimed the slingshot at Mo. "You can tell him."

"Oh, no," Mo said. "I've seen enough mayhem in my life. There's no way I'm going to tell him anything. Pete, it's your job."

Peter wilted. "It's not the mayhem you dread. It's the look on his face. If only there were some way to get him more involved here before we pull the plug."

"The baseball is working pretty well," Mo said. "He had fun last night, and even let them go on their date without him. I tried to introduce him to Beth, the new lawyer who came in last week. He wasn't interested, but I haven't given up."

"Good," Pete said. "We'll just step up the game schedule for the team and keep introducing him to women. Sooner or later he's bound to want to be here more than there. What else does he like?"

"He likes to eat," Dave said. "He always ate healthy before. It probably hasn't occurred to him yet that he can eat anything he wants here and never gain a pound."

"Okay," Pete said. "Then we keep him busy playing ball, we run a string of women past him and we feed him everything his heart desires. But do we pull the plug now or not?"

They were silent for a moment, each looking at the others, waiting for an answer.

"I guess not," Mo said, finally, "seeing how nobody wants to tell him. We'll let him work in another couple of visits, and then we'll all tell him together."

"Couldn't we send him a letter?" Dave asked.

Pete grinned. "We're turning into wimps."

"No, we're not," Dave said. "We just want to see the man happy."

Mo looked skeptical. "Do you think it can ever happen?"

Pete rubbed his forehead thoughtfully. "If we really work at it, it can. Greater miracles have come out of heaven, guys. And if we find we can't handle it, we can always go to plan B or C."

"I hate to do that," Mo said. "Maybe we should just send him upstairs for a private consultation."

"We'll consider that, too," Pete said, "if we can't handle it ourselves."

JASON SAT beside the still waters of the lake that sported foot-long bream, but he didn't fish because he'd come here to think. He sat on a natural plant that grew in the shape of a chair, and felt the light swing of it as the breeze whispered across the water.

If only Sabrina could be here, he thought, they could camp out at night and enjoy the spectacle of the stars, which were much brighter here and held less mystery. There were classes where all the mysteries were explained, but he hadn't taken them yet. Sometime soon, he supposed he really should.

His mind drifted to Sabrina and him camping beside the lake, with no fear of snakes or bugs or rodents to sneak up on them. And the temperature was always perfect. Bree would love it.

She'd also love their house, the huge mansion they'd given him on his first day. They told him he could decorate it any way he wanted—spare no expense—but he hadn't even chosen curtains yet. Decorating had been her thing.

He heard footsteps in the grass behind him and turned to see Pete walking barefoot toward him, carrying a fishing pole in one hand and a box in the other. "Hi, Jason," he said. "I brought you something."

"What?" Jason asked.

Peter handed Jason the box, then cast his hook into the water. "Fudge," he said. "It's the best you've ever had. And in the bottom of the pan is some divinity. My mother baked it."

"Your mother?" Jason laughed. "Did they make fudge and divinity when she was alive?"

"No," Pete said, "but she's picked up a lot of things since she's been here. She loves to cook. It's more fun when you don't have to worry about it going to your gut."

"I hadn't thought of that." Jason took a piece and bit into it, and his taste buds exploded. "That's fantastic," he said. "Absolutely! And you're sure I can eat as much as I want and not gain weight?"

"And you won't eat yourself sick, either."

"You're kidding."

"Nope. You've got to start thinking like an angel, Jason. Everything's good here."

Jason sighed and watched him reel the line in. "I know. And I am starting to think like one. Really, I am."

Pete shot him a look that said he wasn't buying. "You're not kidding anybody, Jason. You've only got one foot in heaven. The other's down there with your wife."

Jason didn't say anything, for he couldn't dispute that. When he saw that Peter had caught a fish, he was thankful to divert the saint's attention.

Pete laughed as he brought the two-foot-long fish out of the water and held it up as if posing for a snapshot. "They didn't have fish like this in the Sea of Galilee."

"They didn't have rods like that, either," Jason said.

Pete unhooked the fish and tossed it back in. "Don't be cynical, Jason. It's not an attractive trait."

"Sorry, man," Jason said. "I'm just a little stressed out lately."

"There's no such thing as stress in heaven," Pete said, "so it must be coming from earth. It isn't good for you to keep going there."

"Just a little longer," Jason said. "Then I'll quit."

Peter gave him a long look, then took a piece of fudge and popped it into his mouth. "Don't you have practice soon?"

"Yeah," Jason said. "I was just getting ready to go change. Thanks for the candy. I'll see you later." He started to walk back, and Pete grabbed his rod and reel and followed him.

"That reminds me, Jason. Since you don't seem interested in decorating your house, we've assigned you a decorator. She'll do it for you. We want to help you settle in here. All you have to do is tell her if you don't like something. How's that sound?"

Jason stopped in his tracks. "Don't tell me. She's a heavenly fox with a great body, right?"

Pete shrugged. "Well, she is attractive, now that I think about it. But I chose her for her talent."

"I don't want to be fixed up, Pete. How many times do I have to tell you?"

"She's just decorating your house, Jason. You don't even have to talk to her if you don't want to. We've given her enough information. We just want you to feel more at home."

Jason felt instantly ashamed. "Okay, then. I just don't want this to be a trick."

They walked quietly for a few moments before Peter spoke again. "Jason, are you any closer to accomplishing your mission than you were before?"

Jason stopped again and looked at his feet. "Yeah, I am," he said softly. "The seed's been planted in his mind, and . . . last night they kissed."

"Don't you think they should be left to build this into something viable?"

"Sure," Jason said. "Eventually."

"And what would happen to make you finally let go?"

Jason looked off into the trees skirting the lake and tried to speak around the emotion in his throat. "I guess when they get married."

"That could take months, Jason. We can't give you that much time. We don't think it's good for either you or her."

"I know," he whispered. He met Pete's eyes, saw the kindness there and knew the man had gone way out on a limb on his behalf. But the former disciple had known grief, and he'd known what it was to let go. Jason supposed it was another example of the symmetry of heaven that Peter was on his committee. "I appreciate your being so patient with me," he said. "And I know I can't keep going back indefinitely. All I ask is that, before you cut me off entirely, give me the chance to say goodbye. I promised her that."

"You shouldn't have."

"I know," Jason sighed. "But I did. She begged me, and I couldn't say no. You should see her eyes when they're sad. They reach out to you, grab you right around the heart. . . ." His voice cracked, and he swallowed. "There's got to be some closure this time or neither of us will really be able to go on. Can't you do that for me?"

Pete knew what he meant about those sad eyes, and he found it just as difficult to say no to Jason. "I guess so, Jason. Try to finish your business there soon. We'll let you know when it's got to end."

Jason nodded, unable to reply, and walked to his mansion to get ready for the game that his heart was not in.

SABRINA HAD WORRIED all day about her date with Danny that night, for she didn't yet know what to expect. Would he tell her he'd thought about their relationship and decided it should stay as it was? Or would it be strained as it moved to a new level? Either way, the stress and anxiety almost made her dread it.

And that dread was compounded by the fact that Jason hadn't made an appearance all day. She missed him, and somewhere in the back of her heart, she nursed the growing fear that she had seen him for the last time. What if he couldn't come back now that his job was done? What if he couldn't keep his promise? And what if he could?

The thought that the next visit might be the last almost made her want to tell Danny never mind, that she wasn't going to get involved with him, because that would mean completing Jason's mission. If she held out, didn't do what he wanted, would he be allowed to keep coming to set her on the right track?

She seriously doubted it. No one in heaven was stupid.

She put the finishing touches on her makeup, then checked her watch. It was almost time for Danny to arrive, and he was never late. But tonight she hoped he would be. She wanted to see Jason just once today before she went to dinner with Danny. Where was he? Why was he staying away?

The thought of those angelic groupies hanging around the dugout tightened her heart, and she wondered if Jason was with one of them tonight. If she was a decent person, worthy of him, she would hope he was. After all, if happiness meant falling in love again...

But somehow she couldn't make herself follow through with that thought. Jason was supposed to have been hers, not just until death parted them, but forever. And she was supposed to have been his. Death had taken not only their marriage, but their dreams.

And now she was supposed to start over.

The doorbell rang, and she took a deep breath and hurried down the stairs.

Danny stood leaning against the wall with his hands in his pockets and an amused grin on his face. "The moment of truth arrives," he said.

She smiled tentatively. "What do you mean?"

He came in and she closed the door behind him. "I mean, I've been nervous about this all day, and now I'm here."

Her heart sank, and she knew what he was going to say. This couldn't work. He wasn't interested in her that way. They should keep things as they were.

"Look," she said, "why don't we just forget last night? We don't have to mess this up. I've been thinking, too, and—"

He framed her face with both hands, hushing her, and said, "Don't you dare back out now. Not when you've put me through all this angst. Do you know I've never really been nervous picking a woman up for a date? Do you know that I've never spent that much time thinking about what to say and how to act? But today, I almost lost a client because I couldn't keep my mind on my work."

"I'm sorry, Danny," she said. "Really, I am. This is all just so crazy."

"So crazy it makes all the sense in the world."

His kiss took her completely by surprise, and she felt her trapped breath escaping, loosening the tension she had wound herself in, reassuring her and gently arousing her. His lips were soft, wet, and he kissed her with a patience and sweet gentleness that she might have guessed at if she'd allowed herself to think of it before.

When the kiss broke, she only stared at him, her eyes glimmering with amazement and vulnerability.

"So are you gonna be my girl, or what?" he asked in a whisper.

She swallowed and wondered why her heart hammered so violently. "Do you want me to?"

"I asked you first."

Slowly, she separated from him and dropped onto the couch. He followed and sat down beside her. "This is so weird, Danny. I feel more comfortable with you than I do anyone else. And last night when we kissed . . . and just now . . . my heart still hasn't gone back to normal."

His smile was beginning to fade. "But?"

"No buts," she reassured him. "It's just weird."

"Tell me the truth," he whispered, tipping her face up. "Do you want to pursue this? Or is it something you brought up just because of Jason?"

She sighed and sank back into the cushions, her eyes closed. "I don't know. What about you? Would you ever have kissed me if I hadn't suggested the idea?"

"No," he said, "but that's just testimony to my uncompromising character and strength." He threw her a big, contagious grin. "Truthfully, I had thought about it a lot before, but I felt a strong loyalty to Jason. Last night you lifted that barrier."

"Well, there have been times over the last three years when I've sort of fantasized about what it would be like."

"And was it like thinking about your brother?"

She laughed. "Hardly. But our friendship was so precious to me, and I needed a friend without all the baggage that goes along with romance."

"And now?"

She lifted her eyebrows, trying to decide what had changed. "Now we've already crossed the threshold. We can either go forward or backward. But we can't stay where we are, anyway."

"And there is that pesky plan to consider."

She smiled. "You believe in a divine plan?"

"You bet I do," he said. "And if Jason told you this was it, then who are we to dispute it?"

Again, she laughed, and realized that the tension had gone. "You really want to pursue it?"

"I do," he said, "but I also don't want to scare you off. We can take it slow. It doesn't have to happen overnight."

"Good," she said, breathing relief. "That's the best idea you've had."

"And we can start by going to a movie tonight," he said. "As I see it, we need to get our minds off this for a while, and just have some fun."

"All right," she said. "No argument from me."

THERE WERE CURTAINS hanging when Jason got to his mansion, and the living room was furnished with elaborate, comfortable things that he and Sabrina had only been able to dream of. It looked like a showplace, but it didn't feel like home.

He walked from one room to the other in the elaborate home, marveling at the sudden change, when he heard footsteps behind him.

He turned around and confronted a woman with huge green eyes and short-cropped hair. "Oh, I didn't know you were home!" she said.

He shrugged. "Sorry. I didn't mean to sneak up on you."

She came forward, her hand extended. "I'm Allison Grey," she said. "Your decorator. How do you like what I've done so far?"

He laughed. "Well, it's gorgeous. You sure do work fast."

"That's the beauty of it," she said, her eyes dancing. "I can make choices, and they just appear. If I don't like them, I can change them in a flash. And I don't have to worry about cost." Her eyes widened even more as she gazed at him. "Can you imagine being able to decorate to your wildest dreams and never have to pay for a thing? It's definitely heaven."

He laughed. "Well, you've done a great job."

"Oh, but this is my taste," she said. "Not yours. And this really should be your choice. If you want me to erase everything and start over..."

"No," he said. "It's all probably stuff I would have picked, anyway." He walked to the living room sofa, made of a fabric superior to anything that could be found on earth, and ran his hand along the back. "My wife would have loved this, too. She always had a flair for decorating. We were fixing up an old house with lots of antiques...."

"Antiques, of course," Allison exclaimed, as if she'd committed a major faux pas. "This stuff is too modern, isn't it?"

When he'd turned around, the dining room table that had previously been made of black lacquer was now more ornate and antique. "How'd you do that?" he asked.

She laughed. "You could do it, too, if you really wanted to. Is that better?"

He shrugged. "Well, yeah, I think so. That's nice. Bree would have loved the hutch. Look at the carving on the door." He moved closer and touched the wood grain with admiring fingertips. "We had one similar to this, but it wasn't this intricate."

"Good, I'm glad you like it," she said. "Now, let's look at the bedroom."

Instantly, he grew tense. "That's okay. Whatever you put is fine. I have to change for a game, anyway."

She put her hands on her little hips and cocked her head. "How new are you?"

He frowned at the oddly worded question. "Three years, earth time. Why?"

"Hmm," she said with a shrug. "You've been here longer than I have. But you still haven't let go, have you?"

He felt a lecture coming on and said, "Look, I don't need this."

"Okay," she said, raising her hands innocently. "I'm sorry. It's just...there's so much wonder here. So much joy. Don't you ever get lonely, thinking only about what was?"

He nodded. "Yeah, sometimes."

"You don't have to be," she said, and he realized it wasn't a come-on, but genuine concern. There was no game-playing in heaven. Just grass-roots honesty. "You know, there is something they can do for you," she said. "They can wipe out your memories, if they get in your way. And then you'd be free to enjoy heaven."

Jason shook his head. "You don't understand. My memories *are* heaven."

"Heaven isn't sad."

"The only thing sad is that my wife is down there, floundering around trying to start a new life, when I had promised her she'd grow old with me."

For a long moment, she looked at him with understanding and compassion in her eyes, probably the very traits that had gotten her here in the first place, and he knew instantly that he liked her. She could be his friend, and maybe he needed a few more friends.

"She'll be okay, Jason," she said, with more familiarity than he had offered her, but it didn't seem alien. "It's all part of the plan. She had to be widowed to be who she is today."

"I know."

For a moment, she only looked at him. "Look, didn't you say you had a game?"

"Yeah."

"Are you any good?"

He laughed. "Amazingly so."

"Then I'll come watch," she said. "And afterward, maybe you can buy me a cup of coffee and we can talk about landscaping."

He gave her a confused look. "Wow. I can't wait."

"How do you feel about swimming pools?" she asked. "And would you like a fountain? Maybe a waterfall in the backyard?"

Laughing, he left her talking in his living room and changed for the game.

Chapter Eight

The ecstasy of his two home runs was short-lived, and minutes after the game ended, Jason checked his watch and wondered if Bree would be home from her date yet.

"Hey, great game, buddy." Don Drysdale patted Jason on the back.

"Thanks, man."

"You want to go get something to eat?"

Ordinarily, Jason wouldn't have passed up the invitation, but his mind was on other things tonight. "Sorry, man, but I have to be somewhere. Maybe next time."

"Sure. See you later, all right?"

"Yeah. Later."

He watched as Drysdale went into the cluster of players signing autographs and posing for pictures with the angelic fans. But it didn't occur to Jason to join them.

Mentally, he calculated the length of the movie they had gone to see, plus the possibility of Sabrina and Danny getting a bite to eat afterward. By now, they should be back, and Danny should be leaving her soon, since they both had to get up early the next morning.

But that hadn't mattered when he and Sabrina were dating. He couldn't help remembering the nights when he'd started to leave at ten, only to get caught in his goodbyes. By eleven, they would realize they had kissed an hour away, and then they'd laugh and talk for an hour more. Twelve would pass and he'd still be there, and by twelve-thirty he'd start his goodbyes again. By one-thirty, if he was lucky, he'd be on his way home.

They'd been tired all the time, but not tired enough to sacrifice time together.

Dolefully, Jason wondered if Sabrina would get that way with Danny. Some part of him, the good, heavenly, pure part, hoped so for her sake. But the other part, the part that hadn't yet let go of his humanity, mourned the fact that she might ever feel that about another man.

"You ready?"

Jason shook himself from his revery and noticed Allison, who'd been walking toward him. "What?"

"Are you ready? You said we'd go get coffee and talk about landscaping."

"No, you said that. I can't go. I have to be somewhere."

She looked at him for a moment, and he saw in her eyes that she knew exactly where he was going. It didn't faze him at all.

"You know, we don't have to talk about landscaping. We could talk about Sabrina if you want to."

Something about her easy familiarity with his wife's name rankled him. "How did you know her name?"

"They gave me your profile so I'd know how to decorate." She grew quiet and tilted her head as he looked away. "Hey, I didn't mean to intrude. Really. I just thought you might need a friend. It isn't easy watching someone you love go on with her life."

He shook his head, unable to pursue this conversation. "I don't want to talk about this."

"Fine," she said. "And you don't want to talk about waterfalls, either? How about mountain ranges? You like those, don't you?"

"Yeah, I like them fine."

"Want the view of one from your backyard? I can do whatever you like."

"Surprise me," he said without much interest. "I really have to go now." He started away, but she stopped him.

"Jason?"

Impatiently, he turned around, and she asked, "Are you going back there for her, or for you?"

For a moment he stared at her, his eyes sharp with resentment. "Did they put you up to this?"

"Who?"

"My committee. Because if they did, it isn't going to work."

"What isn't?"

His eyes were misty as he walked closer to her to make his point. "I'm going to do what I set out to do, and that's to see my wife happy and settled with the right person. And frankly, I don't care what you or anybody else thinks about it."

And without looking back, he stormed away, more unsettled than he'd felt since he'd gotten here.

IT WAS AFTER MIDNIGHT when Danny left. They had gone to a romantic comedy where she'd laughed until she cried, and then he had taken her to Applebees, where they'd had late snacks and laughed some more.

When they got to her house, they had sat on the couch in sock feet and watched David Letterman. It wasn't until he was about to leave that he had kissed her.

"This was the best date I've had in years," he said.

She smiled. "It was nice, Danny."

"I think I like this new concept."

"I think I do, too."

Now she leaned against the door, trying to imagine what it would be like to fall in love with Danny, to commit herself to him, to spend her life with him. The idea held some hope, hope for a family and a full life. But it also held a hint of sadness, for it wasn't her original dream. It wasn't how it was supposed to have turned out.

She sighed and started up the stairs, and when she saw Jason sitting at the top, hunched over in the shadows, she shouted, "Jason!" and ran the remaining steps. "Where have you been?"

He grinned and looked at her as she knelt on the step beneath him. In all the time he'd spent in heaven, he still couldn't think of one thing there that was more beautiful than she. "Oh, I've been here and there."

"I've looked for you all day," she said, her eyes glistening. "I've missed you."

"Yeah, well. You were kind of busy. Big date and all. How'd it go?"

"Fine." He smelled freshly showered, and looked just shaven, and she breathed in his scent and longed to touch his smooth jaw before the stubble started to appear.

"I didn't come here to hear 'fine,'" he said. "You'll have to do better than that."

She noted the irritation in his voice and wondered what was wrong. "Well, we decided to take it slowly. Not put any pressure on ourselves. Just let things happen."

"Aw, man." He got to his feet and stormed into the bedroom as if it were still his and flicked on the light. "I haven't got time for slowly, Bree. I don't have much time left."

She gaped at him, confused. "What do you mean?"

"I mean that they're really breathing down my neck. They're going to stop these visits any time now. I need to see that you're settled before they do, or I'll go nuts, I swear I will."

"But you promised that you'd tell me! You told me—"

"I will, baby," he said, his face looking more distraught than she'd seen lately. "I'll keep that promise. But it'll be soon, don't you see? There isn't time to move slowly."

"But you wouldn't want us to rush into anything. You can't hurry these things."

"It isn't like you don't know him better than anybody else, Bree. You've known him for years. You know that he's got a lot of character, that he's honest and decent and good, that he has the same values as you. You've even had a glowing recommendation from your husband. What else do you need?"

"Love, for one thing!"

"Well, don't you love him?"

She struggled with that for a moment. "Well, of course I love him. As a friend. But it's hard changing my thinking. There's got to be chemistry involved."

"Hey, I saw that kiss tonight. There was definitely chemistry."

Something about his watching them disturbed her, but she let it go. "All right, there is some. But that doesn't mean I'm ready to tie the knot. You wouldn't want me to hurry into a thing like marriage, would you?"

He dropped onto the bed, feeling more helpless and frustrated than he could ever remember being. "No, I don't," he whispered finally. "It's just that I'm getting all this pressure."

"What kind of pressure?"

"They're trying to distract me. Getting me on the team, keeping me busy with practice and games, decorating my house, baking me food, introducing me to..."

She waited for him to go on, but when he didn't, she said, "Introducing you to more women?"

"Yeah," he said. "I told you."

"Are you seeing that lawyer?" she asked.

For a moment he couldn't remember who she was talking about, and then it dawned on him. "Oh, her. No. The decorator is the latest. She—"

"What decorator?" Her voice was too small.

"The one doing the house. Oh, Bree, you'd really love it. All the stuff we couldn't afford here, handcrafted by the masters. It's really all in your taste, too. They knew I liked your taste, so they kind of copied it for me."

She couldn't stop the tears filling her eyes. "And so you've gotten to know this decorator pretty well?"

He looked at her strangely, then said, "Well, no. I hardly know her at all. Hey, don't worry, baby. Whatever their intentions in sending her, you're still the only woman on my mind."

Her nose reddened by degrees as she fought to hold back her tears. "But that isn't healthy, Jason," she whispered. "You need to go on, too. *I* need to know that *you're* happy."

"Would it really make you happy to know that I'm with another woman?" he asked softly.

She thought for a moment, honestly trying to decide. "As happy as it would make you to see Danny and me together."

There. It was out, and as ambiguous as it was, it was honest. For a long moment, he stared at her, his eyes outlined in anguish.

"Why do you look so sad when I say that?" she whispered. "Is it because that really won't make you happy?"

He shrugged and tried to focus on the ceiling. "If fantasies could come true, if deepest wishes could happen, if heaven could be custom-made, I guess I'd have to admit that the thing that would make me happiest would be having you there with me."

She wiped the tear stealing down her cheek and said, "I wish you had never left."

For a long moment, they were silent, lost in their separate but equal fantasies. When Jason spoke again, his voice was soft, dreamlike. He pulled in a deep breath and said, "You should see it, Bree. There's this lake with the stillest waters you've ever seen, and it's full of fish, and these plants that grow in the shapes of hammocks and easy chairs, and you can sit there for hours listening to the music of the breeze."

The rapt twinkle in her eyes was all the encouragement he needed to go on.

"Remember how we used to camp out at Jefferson Park, and rent those paddleboats, and we'd get eaten by mosquitoes? Well, there aren't any mosquitoes in heaven, and if we slept out there, we wouldn't even need a tent. And the night sky... the stars are so vivid, and when they fall, you can see where they land, where they burn out. And you can smell them and touch them, and take them home if you want."

"Why aren't you there instead of here, Jason?" she whispered.

The exuberance in his eyes faded, and he looked at her and shook his head helplessly. "Because I still love you so much."

She caught her breath with a sob and covered her face with her hands, and he wanted with all his soul to touch her. But things were too shaky, and if he did, he knew without a doubt that it would all be over.

Slowly, he pulled back the covers on her bed—their bed. "Come lie down, baby," he whispered. "I'll lie with you until you fall asleep."

Wiping her face, she did as he said and felt him stretching out beside her. There was something terribly wrong with their lying so close without touching. "We never lay like this before," she said.

He wiped his eyes. "I know."

"We used to sleep all tangled up. I'd have my head on your chest, and my leg thrown over your thigh, and you'd have your arms around me and your chin in my hair."

He couldn't imagine her sleeping like that with Danny, but he tried to hope that she would someday. She needed that. She deserved it.

"Good night, sweetheart," she whispered, turning on her side and gazing at him with eyes so wet and big that they made his heart burst.

"Sleep well, baby," he said.

SABRINA BALANCED the grocery sack on one hip and reached into her purse with her free hand to find her house key. Through the door she heard the phone ringing, and finally she jammed the key into the lock. Dropping her purse and the groceries on the counter, she grabbed the phone. "Hello?"

"You're out of breath."

Instantly, she recognized Steven's voice. "I just walked in."

He hesitated, then said, "Bad timing, huh? What else is new?"

Sabrina pulled a chair out from the table and dropped into it, but she didn't answer.

"I guess you're still mad about the other night, huh?"

"That was uncalled-for, Steven, and you know it."

"Yeah, I know," he admitted. "But I was depressed, and I—I guess I had too much to drink."

"That would be my guess, too."

"Well, I called to apologize. I'm really sorry. I made a fool out of myself."

"Yes, you did."

Obviously, her answer took him by surprise. "Well, I hope you'll forgive me."

She sighed, then closing her eyes, said, "Yeah, sure. I don't want to be your enemy."

"Good." The word was spoken with sincerity, and was followed by a tense pause. Then finally, "Tomorrow night would have been our wedding, you know."

She nodded. "My birthday."

Quiet again. "Well, you know what they say about the best laid plans of mice and men." He cleared his throat, then asked, "So how are you doing? I mean, really?"

"Really, I'm fine, Steven. How about you?"

"I'll live. Even though I'm the laughingstock of all my friends."

She felt that old ire rising again. "I'd say you need to get some new friends."

"Well, I can't get a new mother. And she's still ready to kill someone."

"Probably me," Sabrina said.

He laughed, but there was no warmth there. "Yeah, I guess so. Sabrina, I don't want to end this. Maybe it wasn't time for us to get married, but that doesn't mean we have to break up entirely."

"Yes, it does, Steven," she said. "It wasn't right."

"Is that what he told you?"

"Who?"

"Danny? Has he been filling your head with ideas? Because if he has it's only because he's hot for you himself. I've known it from the beginning. That's why I didn't like him."

She changed ears and shifted in her seat. "No, Steven. He hasn't filled my head with ideas. You and I just weren't meant to be together. I believe in destiny. I believe there's a plan. For you, too, you know. If you'd married me, you would have cheated yourself out of the right person."

"Yeah, right," he said balefully. "Look, for old times' sake, why don't you let me take you out to dinner tomorrow night? I want you to celebrate your birthday in style."

"No," she said. "That wouldn't be a good idea, Steven."

"Why not? Do you hate me, when a week ago you were getting ready to marry me?"

"No, but there's no use confusing the issue. We're not going to get back together."

"Then you'd rather sit at home on your birthday than to be with me?"

"Who says I'll be sitting at home?"

For a moment he was quiet, then finally, he said, "That's it, isn't it? You're going out with Danny? He is coming on to you, isn't he?"

"He's been a perfect gentleman."

"That didn't answer my question."

"Exactly."

They endured a long moment of quiet. "You were supposed to marry me tomorrow night, Sabrina, and now you can't even have a conversation with me. We would have been packing for Vienna right now. Welcoming relatives into town. Planning our future together."

Tears came to her eyes, and she whispered, "I'm sorry, Steven. I don't mean to be insensitive. I just...I can't see any reason to keep seeing each other."

"Well, I guess that about sums it up, doesn't it?" She heard the emotion in his voice as he said, "Happy birthday."

And then he hung up.

Slowly Sabrina dropped the phone in its cradle, and pulling her feet into her chair, set her chin on her knees. Tomorrow night she would have been married. Then all this decision-making, all this loneliness, all this grief would have been behind her. And she would never have to be lonely again.

Now she was caught up in the cycle again, of building a new relationship, staring at the stark reality of her future without Jason, hoping for the best. When all the time all she wanted was for things to be back like they were. If she could have just one more chance to live those happy times again, she knew she would never, ever take them for granted.

But it was too late.

A knock sounded on the back door, and wiping her tears, she went to answer it.

Danny stood there, still wearing his suit, with his tie loose and his coat hooked on a finger over his shoulder. His smile collapsed into concern the moment he saw her. "You're crying." He came in and closed the door behind him. "What's wrong?"

"Nothing. Steven just called."

His face reddened as he draped the coat over a chair. "He got you all upset. What did he want?"

"Just to ask me to dinner," she said. "I turned him down."

Taking her hand, he pulled her close and wiped her tears with his fingertips. "Why are you crying?"

"Because," she whispered. "I guess everything's just catching up with me. I was supposed to get married tomorrow night. And all my problems were supposed to be over."

"But you know they wouldn't have been."

She smiled weakly. "Yeah, I know, but it was a nice fantasy."

"Instead of getting married, you'll just have a terrific birthday."

"How can it be terrific?" she asked with a laugh. "I'm turning thirty."

"Yeah, but you don't look a day over twenty-nine and eleven months."

She smiled. "Thanks a lot."

"Truthfully," he said. "You look even better than you did when I met you in college. You get better every year."

"If only I got wiser," she whispered.

He tilted his head and made her look at him. "What does that mean?"

"It means that I should never have gotten involved with Steven. It only hurt us both."

"Steven will be fine. And so will you. And instead of sitting around moping about the wedding tomorrow night, we're going to have a party."

"A party? Where?"

"My house," he said, his grin slipping into his eyes. "Anna's taking care of the catering, today I hired a band, and all I need from you is your list of wedding guests. I don't think any of them are going to be busy tomorrow night."

She grinned. "You wouldn't invite them, really, would you?"

"Why not?" he asked seriously. "Well, I wouldn't invite Steven's friends. He might show up, and then I'd have to kill him. It wouldn't be pretty. But *our* friends would love it."

She smiled at the word "our." "We do have all the same friends, don't we?"

He touched her face and said, "There's no end to what we have in common, Sabrina. This couldn't be more right. Now go throw on a pair of jeans and let me take you out for a hamburger. And then we can go over to my place and you can help me straighten up for the party."

She smiled, feeling better already. "Nope. No hamburgers. Tonight I'm cooking for you. Then we'll go to your place, and see if we can get Felony and Misdemeanor to help us with the house."

THE CAKE was too big to carry, so Jason wheeled it out of the bakery on a special cart, smiling at how well it had turned out. His father had taken him there to introduce him to one of the world's finest bakers, someone who had worked on earth as a cafeteria cook. Jason had labored over the flavor and kind of cake he wanted, and finally, impatient with his indecision, his father had hurried away to meet his friends at the beach for a day of surfing.

When he'd finally placed the order, Jason watched the cake being decorated by a child with more talent than the greatest artist on earth. It looked worthy of a museum when it was finished, yet the smell was too tempting. It had to be eaten. Bree was going to love it.

He wheeled it down the white marble sidewalk, his mouth watering. But he wasn't going to touch it. Not until she saw it first.

"Hey, Jason, how's it going?"

He looked up to see Mo coming toward him, his sandles slapping against his heels.

"I haven't seen you in the marketplace in a long time," Mo said, pleased. "Things must be going well."

"Yeah," Jason said. "I had to buy a cake. Isn't this the most gorgeous thing you've ever seen?"

Mo looked down at the edible gold script that said, "Happy Birthday, Bree." Alarm twisted his face. "Wait a minute. You aren't planning to take this to her, are you?"

Jason shrugged. "Well, yeah. It's her birthday. Her thirtieth, and she's been kind of bummed, considering what she's been through lately, and—"

"That doesn't matter," Mo cut in. "You can't take her food from heaven!"

"Why not? You lived on manna for years."

"That was different. We were starving, and it was food from God. You can't make the decision on your own to sneak her food from here."

"For Pete's sake, it's just a cake."

"I don't care whose sake it's for, you can't do it!" Mo returned. "You're really pushing it, Jason. You know better."

Jason dropped his hands to his sides. "Well, then what am I supposed to do with it? Somebody worked really hard on it. Am I supposed to just throw it away?"

"Have a party," Mo suggested hopefully. "I'll bring the wife, if she's not dancing in the ballet tonight, and we'll invite the team and some of the nice young ladies you've met recently."

Jason knew that if he throttled the man, he'd probably get tossed right out of heaven. Trying to restrain himself, he said, "I don't want a party, Mo! It's my wife's birthday, and I want to celebrate with her."

"Her friends will help her celebrate," Mo said. "She's in good hands. You can celebrate here."

"I'm not hanging around here on my wife's birthday, man." His face reddened, and his teeth came together. "Whether I take her the cake or not, I'm going to be with her."

"But you have a game tonight," Mo said. "Did you forget about that?"

Jason hesitated. "They can do without me this once, Mo. This is important."

"Absolutely not," Mo said. "I insist that you go to the game. What you do after it is up to you, but you have to keep your commitments here first."

"Great," Jason said. "She'll turn thirty without me."

He started to walk away, but Mo caught him. "I thought the whole purpose of your going back was to turn her over to your friend."

"What if Danny doesn't do the right thing? What if he doesn't even know it's her birthday? The guy was terrible with dates. He forgot his own birthday if somebody didn't remind him!"

"Give him a chance, Jason. The world will go on without you. *Her* world will go on without you. If you truly love her, you'll let it."

Jason's eyes were misty as he shook his head. "You just don't understand," he said. "You got to grow old with your wife."

Mo dropped his hand, knowing he couldn't argue with that. With a defeated slump, Jason walked away, leaving him with the cake that had been made in vain.

THE BAND set up in Danny's living room launched into its rendition of "Your Mama Don't Dance." In his dining room, from which all the furniture had been cleared to make room for the dance floor, fifty or more people danced.

From his den, where others talked and laughed, Sabrina caught a glimpse of Danny. He was wearing a sheet on his head, wound up like a turban, and he was doing his psychic tricks, guessing what people had in their pockets. Everyone around him was in stitches.

His laughing eyes caught hers, and he winked. Sabrina smiled.

"Okay, that's it." Anna dropped her plate of hors d'oeuvres and grabbed Sabrina's arm. "I saw that look, and I demand an explanation."

"What look?" Sabrina asked innocently as Anna dragged her through the swinging door to the kitchen.

Anna pushed Sabrina into a chair and leaned over her like an interrogator. "All right, Sabrina. Give me the lowdown. What's going on with you and Danny?"

Sabrina laughed and took an hors d'oeuvre off a tray that hadn't been served yet. "I don't know what you mean."

"Maybe my fingers around your throat can help you remember," Anna said. "Something's going on with you two. Now tell me!"

Sabrina shrugged and popped the delicacy into her mouth. "Well, maybe a little something."

Anna's eyes widened like saucers, and she grabbed her shoulders. "Are you two becoming an item? Is that why you broke up with Steven?"

She laughed again. "No, Anna. He's not why I broke up. But as for us becoming an item ... Well, let's just say that we're sort of experimenting with being more than friends."

"That's wonderful!" Squealing, Anna threw her arms around her friend. "I've always thought the two of you would make a perfect couple, but one time I mentioned it to him, and he said he could never betray Jason's memory. I tried to tell him that it wouldn't be a betrayal, but I finally decided it was hopeless. Whose idea was it, anyway?''

Sabrina turned to the hors d'oeuvres and matter-of-factly answered, ''Jason's.''

Anna looked amused, but she drew her brows together. ''Now there's a new twist. Well, however it happened, I'm glad it has. Oh, this is going to be so perfect. He's so much better for you than Steven.''

''Anna, don't get carried away. We're just testing the waters.''

''I know, but I just—''

The door swung open, and Anna stopped cold as Danny ambled in, holding his makeshift turban in his hands. He looked from Sabrina to Anna and back again, that grin twinkling in his eye. ''I sense that I'm interrupting something.''

''Wow, you're good,'' Anna said. ''We were just talking about you, as a matter of fact.''

''Oh?'' Danny chuckled and tossed a kernel of popcorn into his mouth. ''Well, then I guess she told you she's pregnant with my twins and that we're getting secretly married tonight after the party. That drummer guy out there with the beard is the minister.''

Anna laughed and slapped his stomach. ''You devil. If you'd just listened to me a year ago...''

Danny knew what she referred to, and he met Sabrina's eyes.

"I'm gonna leave you two alone," Anna said in a mother-hen tone. "I have some hors d'oeuvres to serve." Grabbing the tray, she pushed out of the kitchen, that silly grin still planted on her face.

"I take it she approves," Danny said.

Sabrina nodded. "I think you could say that."

"Then it's unanimous." He pulled her out of the chair and slid his arms around her. "Has anyone told you you're the prettiest birthday girl here tonight?"

"No," she said, smiling at him. "I don't think anyone has."

"Well, then, let me be the first." The laughter in his eyes receded, giving way to a more serious twinkle. "You're not only the prettiest, but there's something that just radiates from you. I've seen it since I first met you. That first time Jason brought you home when we were roommates, and I took one look at you and thought he was the luckiest guy in the world."

She swallowed the emotion rising in her throat. "You're sweet."

"No, I'm honest," he said. "And I've been thinking about all this. A lot." He hesitated, choosing his words carefully. "And the truth, Sabrina, is that I don't think I can take it slow. I know you better than any man could hope to know the woman he chooses. There's no doubt in my mind that you're in my plan. And I have to tell you that the idea of marriage and children with you sounds really good to me.''

Her smile faded, and she felt her heartbeat stumble. "This isn't a proposal, is it?"

"Not if you don't want it to be," he said softly. "I don't want to rush you or scare you. And if you don't want to hear talk like this, then tell me, and I'll shut up. But I've been looking for the right woman all my life, and now I know she's been under my nose all along. I don't want to waste another day."

Her eyes filled with wonder, and she struggled to find the right words. But they wouldn't come.

His kiss let her off the hook, but as he held her, touching her, loving her as Jason could no longer do, a profound sadness rose in her heart. And for the life of her, she didn't know where it came from.

He broke the kiss, then grazed her lips with a whisper touch. "Are you having a good birthday?"

She nodded.

"Well, then, let's go dance. People are going to start talking if we don't come out of here soon."

But as they pushed through the swinging door, he kept his arm around her shoulder. And Sabrina knew that by the end of the night, there wouldn't be a doubt among them that Danny and Sabrina were a couple.

She was the only one who had doubts.

Chapter Nine

Jason didn't find Sabrina at home on her birthday, and since he hadn't been able to get there earlier that day, he had no idea what plans she'd made. When it finally occurred to him to try looking for her at Danny's, he popped into the yard and he saw the band loading the last of its equipment, and Anna and a couple of others driving away.

A party, he thought suddenly. Danny had thrown her a party. He should have known his friend wouldn't let her down.

He wondered if there had been a cake.

He went into the house, not making a sound, and saw Danny and Sabrina dancing to a song on Danny's CD player. Danny was spinning her, dipping her and making her laugh the way she used to laugh with him. She was having fun.

Smiling, Jason stepped into the shadows.

The song ended, and Sabrina collapsed onto the arm of the sofa. "Come on. I'll help you clean up."

"No way," Danny said. "You're the birthday girl. You can't help me clean up. That's against the bylaws. It's a breach of contract. It's a travesty. I can't allow it."

She laughed lightly at his melodrama.

"But this is a mess! You were so sweet to give me a party, the least I can do is help you."

"Tell you what," Danny said. "You go home and get some sleep, and then tomorrow you can come back and help me. I'll leave it until then, I promise."

"Are you sure?"

"Yes," he said. "It's a good way to get you over here tomorrow." Taking her hand, he pulled her to her feet. Sliding his arms around her, he said, "You know, I meant what I said tonight. I don't want to take this slowly."

Her smile faded as she gazed into his eyes. "I know, Danny, but it's just so weird. I'm not used to the idea yet, and I don't want to—I can't jump into anything."

Danny let her go, crestfallen. "Tell me the truth, Sabrina. Do you see any possibility for a future with me?"

"Of course I do," she said. "That's why I brought it up in the first place. I believe you're a part of the plan, Danny."

"Jason wouldn't kid about that," Danny assured her. "The man knows what he's doing."

"I know he does."

Danny closed his arms tighter around her, and she laid her head on his chest and closed her eyes. "You know, I think I've loved you for a real long time," he said. "I just couldn't admit it until I had Jason's approval."

She looked at him and touched his face with curious fingertips, but her eyes were serious. "Has anybody ever told you you're a wonderful man?"

The fact that she didn't return his confession of love didn't seem to faze Danny, but Jason recognized it right away. And as they kissed, he stepped farther back into the shadows, turned his head away and closed his eyes. That kind of thing just wasn't easy to watch.

He didn't look again until Danny had walked her to her car, kissed her goodbye again, then come back in.

Danny locked the door and leaned against it, smiling with glistening eyes, and for the first time since he'd met his best friend, Jason envied him with all his heart.

"Things are going pretty well, hey, buddy?" Jason asked.

He knew Danny couldn't hear, but it didn't matter. There were things that had to be said anyway. Danny pushed away from the door, went into the living room and started stacking paper plates. Jason followed him.

"You know, I wouldn't want her with anybody but you," Jason went on. "I know you'll take good care of her. I know you'll make her happy."

Danny dropped the stack of plates into a garbage bag, then dropped into his favorite recliner, staring into space. There was no doubt in Jason's mind that his friend was thinking of Sabrina, reliving every word she'd said to him tonight, recalling every touch, remembering every smile. He didn't blame him. He did it himself, all the time.

Jason sat down on the coffee table in front of Danny, facing him.

"You see, buddy, I'm just having a hard time with this. She's so precious to me, and... It's nothing you're doing. Nothing at all. I just don't know how I'm gonna let go of her."

Danny dropped his elbows onto his knees and looked at the floor, the pleasure in his eyes giving way to melancholy, as if some part of Danny sensed what Jason was saying.

"It's just that she's the most loving person I've ever met," Jason went on, his voice cracking. "Did you know that a day didn't go by when I was here that she didn't meet me at the door with a kiss and a wonderful, sweet hug when I got home? Did you know that I never left for work without her kissing me goodbye? And the thing is... I just can't imagine her going through life without someone else to do that for. And if it can't be me, then I want it to be you."

He wiped his eyes and tried to steady his voice, even though it didn't matter. Danny couldn't really hear him.

He took in a deep breath and tried to go on. "So I'm gonna do something for you, Danny, old buddy. I'm gonna say goodbye to her." He dropped his face, covered it with his hands, and Danny finally sat up and leaned back in the chair, his face pensively sad, almost as if he knew what Jason was saying.

"Only...I can't do it tonight, because it's her birthday, and I don't want her sad on her birthday."

Jason tried to stop his tears, because he'd never been comfortable with them, but they kept coming. Wiping them roughly away, he said, "I'll do it tomorrow night. And after that, you won't have to keep sharing her with me. She'll be free to concentrate on you, and fall in love, and plan a future. And without me in the way, it'll be perfect, Danny. I know it will."

For a moment the two men sat silently, Danny staring into space, Jason slumped on the coffee table. Finally, Jason stood up and started for the door. "See you later, pal. Take good care of my baby."

He stopped at the door before leaving, and turned back. "And thanks for throwing her the party, man. I always meant to do that for her. Just never got around to it."

And then he disappeared through the door, and left Danny with the quiet, conflicting feelings coursing through him.

"LET'S TALK about this cake incident." Pete's voice was dryer than usual, and Jason sensed his displeasure. That, no doubt, was why he'd been summoned to this committee meeting. Mo had ratted on him.

"It was just a cake," Jason said. "It's not like I was going to change history or create a natural disaster or anything. A stupid cake for my wife's birthday."

"But you knew better," Dave said.

"I didn't do it, okay? Mo stopped me."

"But don't you see why we're concerned? If you'll consider doing that, we're afraid you'll do other things. You're crossing the line, Jason. You're getting out of control."

"Jason, we have reasons for what we do," Dave said. "If you had taken it to her, you *would* have interfered in her life. She would have chosen to be with you rather than going to the party Danny gave her, and that party was an important bonding event for them."

"Well, you don't have to worry about that anymore, okay?" Jason sprang up and stalked across the room. "You all know I promised Danny last night that I'd say goodbye to her. Isn't that what you want?"

"We want to make sure you do. Danny didn't really hear you say that. He can't hold you to it."

"He knows," Jason said with certainty. "I felt it. Somehow, he got it. And I made the decision on my own, not because you forced me to."

"We do applaud you for that," Mo said. He leaned forward at the table and studied Jason's face. "Why *did* you come to that decision?"

Jason sank down. "I finally realized that what you've been saying is true. She can't go on with this until I'm out of the picture. I wanted to see it through, but at this point, it doesn't really matter what I want. It's her happiness that's important."

"Her happiness is being taken care of, Jason," Pete said, his voice softening. "It's yours that concerns us. Nothing we've done has made you happy yet."

"I know," Jason said, "but that's not my concern right now. She is." He leaned forward in his chair, his eyes focused on each of them in turn. "But I had this idea. I can say goodbye to her tonight, just like I promised, but I want permission to keep returning to her as her guardian angel. Permanently. That way, I can always keep an eye on her, but she won't know I'm there, and she'll be free to fall in love with Danny and build a life with him."

"That won't make you happy," Dave said. "It'll make you miserable, always watching her with another man. We can't allow that."

"It's the *only* thing I can see that'll make me happy," Jason said. "Think about it, guys. I'm not asking that you give me a kingdom or anything selfish like that. I'm asking for service...service to her. Somebody's got to do it."

"Not you," Peter said sadly. "I'm sorry, Jason, but we can't allow that."

Jason sat back in his chair, his eyes reddening. "All right then, I have another idea. I want you to put me to sleep until she comes here."

"What?" Mo asked. "Why would you want to sleep decades away when you're in *heaven?* You could be enjoying your eternity. Everything you could ever want is here."

"Not everything," he said. "And until she is here, I don't have much use for any of it." He sighed and went on. "I've thought this out, and I realize that she'll be Danny's wife when she finally grows old and dies, and probably by then he'll be the one she feels the most married to. And I can live with that, too. Just put me to sleep until that time comes, and once she's here, I'll be happy just being near her."

The three men passed meaningful looks among each other, none of which escaped him, and finally Pete steepled his hands in front of his face and settled his solemn eyes on Jason.

"Son, I know you feel like you know what'll make you happy, but I don't think either of these plans will do that. You deserve happiness. That's why you're here." He glanced at the other two and shrugged. "I don't know about you guys, but I'm at a loss. I think Jason needs a private consultation. Jason, we're going to send you upstairs."

Jason's eyes widened. "Really? You mean He can take time out of running the universe to talk to me?"

"Of course He can," Pete said. "And He'll know what to do."

Jason was smiling as he left the room, and suddenly he felt hopeful that things were going to work out. All he had to do was explain his predicament, and he'd have the permission he needed.

PETE WATCHED JASON leave the room, then turned solemnly to Mo and Dave, who sat in quiet contemplation, waiting for him to speak. "What do you think He'll decide?"

"The same thing we would have. Not to let him go back and not to put him to sleep," Mo said. "Let's face it. Whether Jason likes it or not, we have no choice but to go with Plan B and erase his memory. This is the worst case of memory-clinging I've ever seen."

Dave nodded. "As much as I hate to do that, I think it's the only way, too. Otherwise, he has no chance of ever being happy."

Pete sighed heavily and ran his hand over his crew cut. "Well, let's see what comes out of his consultation. We'll know for sure what to do then."

"What about this goodbye he's planning?" Dave asked. "Should we let him go?"

"We have to," Mo said. "He made a promise, and we agreed to allow it. But it won't be easy for him."

"No, it won't," Pete said. He sat back helplessly in his chair, rubbing his tired eyes. "I hate to think of the pain it'll put him through."

"Or her pain," Dave said. "She'll grieve his loss all over again."

"We can only blame ourselves," Pete said. "Maybe we should have never let him go."

"He's an awfully persuasive guy," Mo said. "That's why he was such a good lawyer."

Dave slid his chair back. "Not persuasive enough to convince Him to go along with his ideas, though."

"You never know." Pete got up and headed for the door. "His compassion sometimes makes Him change His course. Let's just wait and see."

THE COMMITTEE was waiting for him at the bottom of the stairs when Jason came out of his consultation. The fact that he glowed brought smiles to the three men's faces. In all his life, he'd never felt more heard and understood, and now he believed that, no matter what, things were going to work out.

"I told you he'd agree with me," Jason said as the men came to their feet.

Mo's jaw fell. "He *agreed* with you?"

"Well, sort of," Jason said. "Maybe. He said He'd think it over, and that after I've said goodbye to her, He'd let me know His decision."

The three men grew quiet, for their interpretation was not the same as his. "Jason, that doesn't mean He's going to give you what you asked for."

"It doesn't mean He won't, either," Jason said. "I have to have faith. I have to hope for the best. The great thing was that He understands. He knows."

"Is that a surprise to you?" Dave asked.

"To some extent, I guess it is." Jason looked at them, from one to the other, and his smile faded. "I appreciate you guys being so patient with me. I realize I've been a pain. And you could have made demands and punished me and all sorts of things, but you've been kind and patient and compassionate. Thanks a lot."

Pete touched his shoulder, and his eyes were pained as he looked into Jason's. "This isn't going to be easy for you tonight, Jason. We'll be thinking about you, okay?"

Jason blinked back the emotion already threatening his eyes. "Yeah, sure. It'll be okay." He shook each of their hands, patted their backs and said, "Well, I'd better go get ready."

The three men could think of nothing more to offer him as Jason walked out of their sight.

SABRINA WASN'T SURE why she had asked Danny not to come over that night, but all day she'd had a strong sense that she needed to be alone. Maybe things were just happening too fast, maybe she felt overwhelmed, maybe she had too much to do.

Or maybe it was just that she missed Jason so terribly, and hoped he'd make an appearance if he knew she was alone.

She had spent the morning with Danny, helping him clean up after the party, and then she had come home, caught up on her laundry, straightened her house, organized some art projects for her class during the coming week. Now she sat alone in the living room, her lights turned low, waiting, waiting....

She felt his presence before she saw him, and stood up. "Jason?"

As he came into the room, she saw the sad, solemn look on his face. "Yeah, baby, it's me."

"I've been waiting for you. Where have you been? I haven't seen you for days, and I was afraid..."

"I told you I'd be back," he said. "Didn't I?"

She nodded. "But I expected to see you on my birthday."

He smiled. "Yeah, well, you did all right without me. I was gonna bring you a cake, but... I was there, you know. I saw the party, and you and Danny..."

"You were hurt," she whispered. "That's why you didn't come to me."

"No," he said. "I'm happy that Danny wants to move faster. That's what I wanted. Really. And that's why I kind of had a talk with Danny last night."

She frowned. "He didn't tell me that. Did you appear to him?"

"No," he said. "But I said what I had to say. And I think it reached him. Not audibly, but it sank in somehow."

She walked closer to him, looking at him, and reaching up to almost touch his face. But she stopped herself. "What did you say?"

His eyes twinkled with pain as he gazed at her. "I told him . . . that tonight I would come and tell you goodbye."

A heartbeat didn't pass before tears assaulted her, and she sobbed on a broken breath. "No, Jason. It's not time!"

"It is time, baby. It's long past time."

"But I still need you. Things aren't right yet, Jase, and I need you to—"

"You don't need me, baby," he said, his eyes intently holding her even if his hands couldn't. "What you need is for me to let you get on with your life."

"What life?" she shouted. "This isn't life! This is hell, and I haven't even died yet!"

"It's not hell, baby. It's gonna be all right. You're in good hands. Danny will make you happy."

"But *you* made me happy!" she sobbed. "Why couldn't I have you?"

"Because it wasn't in the plan."

"Then the plan was wrong!"

Her anguish was more than he could bear, more than he'd ever imagined, and he gave in to his own tears. "Baby, listen to me."

"I can't!" she sobbed. "Not if you're leaving. Not if you're saying goodbye."

"You asked me to, Bree. You begged me not to stop coming without telling you."

"Either way, I lose you again!" she whispered hoarsely. "Either way, you're there and I'm here."

"You'll be there, too, someday," he promised her. "I'll wait for you."

"But it won't be the same, Jason. I'll have a whole lifetime without you, and you'll have part of an eternity without me." Again, she wilted into her tears, holding herself and weeping out the anguish still growing in her heart.

For a moment he stood helpless, staring at her, willing his hands to stay at his sides, not to touch her. And then it occurred to him that there was nothing worse they could do to him. If he couldn't come back, if he couldn't talk to her, then there was little they could take away.

And if they threw him out of heaven for touching her... Well, it would be worth it to stop her tears for just a few minutes.

Slowly, he reached out, and with a trembling hand touched her bowed head. Her hair felt like silk, soft and sleek and baby-fine as he remembered, and instantly she looked up.

He moved his hand around to her neck, and as her tears rolled more freely, she took his palm and kissed it.

"I love you," he whispered. "I'll always love you."

Another sob caught her in its grip, and her brown eyes reddened with the pain of it all.

And then something in him snapped—that last fiber of his control—and he pulled her against him, crushed her into him, buried his face in her hair, breathed in the scent of her natural perfume and marveled at the heaven of her arms around him, clinging, holding, loving...

For a short space of eternity, they wept in each other's arms, and finally, he turned her face up to his. His kiss was wet, scathing, arousing, and she lost herself entirely in it. Her tears kept coming, faster, harder, one part sweet relief, one part pure despair.

"What will they do to you for touching me?" she whispered.

"I don't care," he said. "It doesn't matter."

"Will they punish you?"

"I'm already being punished," he said. "Every time I leave you, I die all over again. Every tear you shed, I feel it all the way in heaven. I think I always will.''

He kissed her again, and this time he lifted her and carried her up the stairs to their bedroom, to their bed, to the place where they had made love so many times, where they'd planned out their family, where they'd dreamed about growing old.

He laid her down on the bed, wanting with all his heart to consummate his love as he had done so many times before. But he knew it would never go that far, for they would stop it. It would be worse than bringing her cake.

Lying down next to her, he held her, and finally she laid her head on his chest and crossed her leg over his thigh, and he held her tight in the circle of his arms, with his face buried in her hair. And together they wept some more.

''I miss you,'' she whispered. ''I miss this. I miss making love. I miss everything about you.''

''I miss it, too, baby.''

''Nobody will ever make me feel the way you do,'' she whispered.

''They'll make you feel different,'' he said. ''Maybe even better.''

''Never.'' She looked at him, touched his face. ''Jason, why would God make two people so perfect for each other, and bring them together, only to take one of them away?''

"I don't know," he whispered. "Maybe there's a reason we just don't understand yet."

He reached down and wiped her tears with his knuckles.

"I realize," she went on, "that I'm not the only one who's ever lost a husband. But the others I know, they seem to go on with their lives. They seem to start over and find ways to be happy again."

"Maybe their spouses aren't haunting them, interfering in all their decisions. Maybe if I hadn't come back, you would have made the right decisions on your own. Maybe I should have just left you alone."

"No," she said, sobbing again. "No, Jason. I'm so glad you came back." Sobs racked her body, and he gathered her closer, as close as she could physically be to him. But their intimacy transcended the physical, and their spirits, for a short time, were one.

When hours had passed, and she had cried herself to sleep in his arms, Jason knew that it was time to go. He had said his goodbye, and he had held her one last time, and now he had to do what he'd promised. Now he had to leave her alone.

Stroking her hair from her forehead, he kissed it, and with tears still in his eyes, whispered, "Bye, baby. I'll never forget you."

Then wiping his eyes, he got out of bed, beheld her sleeping as peacefully as if he were still holding her, and went back to where they said he belonged.

Chapter Ten

They were waiting for him on his veranda when he got back to his house—Mo, Dave and Pete—and sarcastically, Jason held out his wrists. "Go ahead. Cuff me and take me in."

None of them moved. "You're expecting punishment, are you?" Pete asked.

Jason shrugged. "I don't know, and I don't really care. I touched my wife, I kissed her, I held her and I comforted her. And whatever that costs me, I'm willing to pay it."

"We're not here to punish you, Jason." Dave got up and came to the steps leading off the veranda and looked down at him. "We were worried about you."

"Well, there's no need to be. I did what I had to do."

"We weren't worried about you not going through with it, Jason," Mo said quietly. "We were worried about your state of mind after you did it. Are you sure you're all right?"

Suddenly Jason softened, and those tears began to sting his raw eyes again. He blinked them back. "Yeah, I'm fine."

"We want to help you, Jason."

"Then just let me be alone for a while. I appreciate your concern, but...I just want to be left alone."

"If it's any consolation, we were told to tell you that you will be allowed to go back and watch her until she marries again. But your power to appear to her has been taken from you. You can watch her, but she won't know you're there."

He looked at Pete, his sad eyes breaking the saint's heart. "Then the guardian angel idea was denied?"

"Sorry, son."

"And the sleep?"

"I'm afraid not. This is the best we can do."

If it was possible for Jason to look more dejected, he did. "Well, at least I can watch her get married. That's something, I guess." Walking across the veranda, he opened the front door. "Thanks for coming, guys."

They sat there, watching helplessly, as Jason went into his house.

When the door was closed, Pete turned to the others. "After she's married, I don't think we have a choice. We've got to clean his slate."

"Poor guy. This is really hard on him."

"We should give him some kind of reward for putting himself through so much pain for her, though," Dave said. "It's really very moving."

Pete shook his head. "That's just it. Just being near her was reward enough for him."

"He won't be the same person without his memories of her," Dave added.

"No, he won't," Mo agreed. "But he'll be happy. And that is the bottom line in heaven."

THE CHEF HAT that Danny wore coordinated nicely with his Kiss the Chef apron as he flipped hamburger patties and sang "You Ain't Nothin' But a Hound Dog" under his breath, shaking his hips and occasionally using the spatula for a microphone.

Sabrina came to the back door and smiled. The grief she had experienced over the last few weeks was almost as bad as the grief she'd felt when Jason died, but this time she had turned to Danny, for she knew it was what Jason would have wanted. He had understood her renewed sadness and had been there for her. They grew closer than she'd ever imagined, and she found herself loving him more with each passing day.

Tonight they had decided to cook out, and she knew from his mood that something special was in the air. He'd been very patient with her, but now, she suspected, he was ready for their relationship to move forward. Danny was thinking of marriage, she was sure of it. He'd been talking a lot lately about fatherhood and family, and she couldn't say the idea didn't appeal to her. It was a new start, a fresh beginning, and she was so tired of being depressed.

She brought the special sauce he'd made out to him, and he thrust out a hip and, to his spatula, said in his best Elvis voice, "Thank you. Thank you very much."

She laughed in spite of herself, and he set the sauce down and twirled her around. She squealed with delight, and Danny stopped and smiled at her. "Do you know how beautiful you are when you laugh?"

She shook her head. "Tell me."

"So beautiful," he said, "that every angel in heaven points to you when they make their wish list and says, 'I want to look like that.'"

She sighed and tried to push thoughts of Jason in heaven out of her mind. "That's so sweet."

He sat down on a stool and pulled her onto his lap. She nuzzled against him, glorying in the feel of his strong arms around her. "Do you know how much I love you?" he asked softly.

She smiled. "Yes, I think I do. And I love you, too."

He touched her face and made her look at him. "Then what are we waiting for?"

Her smile fell. "I don't know what you mean."

"Why aren't we making wedding plans?"

Her smile was coy as she gazed at him. "Because you haven't officially proposed."

"What do I have to do?" he asked. "Get down on my knees, plead with you, give you a ring?"

She giggled. "Maybe not all of it. But you at least have to ask."

He pulled her off his lap then and stood up. Setting her in his place, he got down on one knee, took off his chef's hat and looked solemnly up at her. "Sabrina, you would make me the happiest man in the world if you would be my wife." He reached into his apron pocket and pulled out a small box. "Please, darlin'. Won't you marry me?"

She gasped as he opened the box and showed her the radiant diamond solitaire. Speechless, she only gaped at it.

He took the ring out, lifted her trembling hand and slid the ring on her finger. "Look," he said. "It fits."

She smiled softly. "Yes, it does. It fits."

"Then it's a done deal?" he asked her.

She smiled. "Yes, Danny. It's a done deal. I would love to be your wife."

A FEW FEET AWAY, Jason sat on the edge of a lawn chair, watching his wife become betrothed to another man. She was finally happy, he thought, and that was a good thing. She finally had a future.

He was happy for both of them. Really he was.

Slowly, he got up, knowing neither of them could see him, and walked away, leaving them alone to celebrate the life they were beginning together.

THE GUEST LIST for her wedding was considerably shorter than it had been with Steven, for the wedding was going to be simple and sweet, and only their closest friends, the ones who knew their history, would be invited.

Sabrina's mother sat over the invitations with her, addressing envelopes and applying stamps, when she looked up at her daughter and asked, "Are you sure this time, Sabrina?"

She smiled. "Of course I'm sure. Just because I almost married the wrong guy once doesn't mean I'll do it again."

"I don't think for a minute that Danny's the wrong guy, honey," she said. "I just want to be sure that you're ready."

"I am, Mom. He makes me laugh. I love him, and I know we'll be happy."

"But are you *in* love with him?"

Sabrina hesitated and tried to put the question in perspective. It was a valid question from a mother who'd seen her daughter go through more than her share of misery. The problem was that Sabrina wasn't sure how to answer it. Sliding her chair back, she got up to pour a cup of coffee.

"The way I felt about Jason was magic, right from the beginning," she said softly. "I'm not sure that feeling happens to everybody. And I know it never happens to the same person twice. It's not possible to love two people that deeply in the same lifetime."

"You didn't answer my question."

Sabrina sighed and brought her cup to the table. "I love Danny," she said. "And he loves me. We'll spend the rest of our lives making each other happy."

Her mother just looked at her for a long moment, then touching her hand, reached over and kissed her cheek. "You're my only daughter, and you've been so sad. I want you to be happy, honey. I want you to experience everything life has to offer."

"I want that, too, Mom," she said. "And I'm going to do everything I can to make it happen." She set down her cup and breathed a heavy sigh. "And to prove that I'm committed to Danny, and that I've stopped clinging to the past, I've decided to sell the house."

"What?" Her mother threw her hand over her heart. "I thought you loved this house. I thought Danny loved it."

"It has a lot of memories," she said, looking around. "But a lot of them are sad. I've shed a lot of tears in this house, Mom. And I've spent a lot of lonely nights here. I want us to start fresh. We'll have a better chance that way."

"Are you sure?"

"Yeah," Sabrina said, but her voice was weak as she said it. "Yeah, Mom, I'm sure."

DANNY WAS AS SOMBER as Sabrina the day they closed the deal on the house. They had stipulated that she was to have a month to move out, and with their wedding only a few days away, they both agreed they could take their time sorting through her things.

But signing those papers wasn't as easy as Sabrina had told herself it would be. She was ashamed of herself when tears assaulted her, but when she looked up to see Danny's eyes full of tears, too, she knew everything was going to be all right. Letting go of the house was hard for him, as well, for it held memories of his best childhood friend.

Later, they sat alone on the front porch swing, holding hands and thinking about what they were doing. "You know, you didn't have to sell," he whispered. "We could have lived here. It would have been fine with me."

"It wouldn't have been fair," she said. "You had to put up with a lot in the beginning, with me still clinging to Jason. I have to let go entirely, Danny. You deserve a woman who's a hundred percent yours."

"But I don't mind sharing you with him. He's sharing you with me. I loved him, too, you know."

"I know," she said. She laid her head on his shoulder and whispered, "Remember when we bought this house? It was in such bad shape."

Danny smiled. "It took a solid month for Jason and me to sand down those floors and polyurethane them. Remember that time the phone rang, and he ran through a wet room and ruined it? We had to start all over."

"We never got the footprints out entirely. They're still there, in the dining room."

"I know," he whispered. "And now I'm glad he made them."

She fought the urge to go in there right now, find the footprints and run her fingertips across them, conjuring up the memory of the despair and disgust on his face.

"Remember when the banister fell off?" Danny asked.

"Yeah. And that fireplace that was here when we bought it. Remember all the trouble we had getting the new one here?"

He laughed. "Yeah. That old house you found it in was almost condemned."

"And we almost couldn't get it out, and then we couldn't get *ours* out."

"And the mantel didn't fit in the back of my truck."

She laughed again. "I had almost given up when you and Jason drove up with that flatbed trailer, and he was standing in the back, literally holding it on."

Their laughter rose and fell together, and finally, Danny whispered, "I'm gonna miss this place."

"Yeah," she said with a sigh. "Me, too."

He looked at her, his eyes as serious as she'd ever seen them. "Are you sure you're doing the right thing by marrying me, Sabrina? Are you sure it's the right thing for you?''

"I'm sure," she whispered, and before he could see the pain in her eyes, she hugged him and buried her face in his neck.

THE NIGHT BEFORE the wedding, Sabrina wanted to be alone. It was the last night she'd actually live in her house, and she wanted a private, quiet goodbye before she left it behind.

Instead of the elation she should have felt before her wedding, she was melancholy, almost sad, but she attributed it to entering a new phase of life and leaving the old one behind. Why did her emotions have to be so complicated, she wondered. Why couldn't things be simple?

Restless, she climbed the stairs to the attic, where Jason's clothes still hung, turned on the light and looked around at the memories she had stored there. Danny hadn't demanded that she get rid of them, as Steven had, and some of them she would keep. But she couldn't keep them all.

She saw the antique mirror standing in the corner, and taking an old rag that lay on a box, she dusted it off until she could see her reflection in it. She was pale, she thought, and she'd gotten too thin. Not like a blushing bride at all. What would Jason have thought of her now?

She didn't see him as he sat on one of the boxes in the corner, watching her quietly, knowing that this was one of the last times he could. Tomorrow, when she married Danny, it would be his last time to steal back to earth. Tonight was all he had with her, and though he was ashamed to admit it, he was glad she'd decided to spend it alone.

He watched as she stared at her reflection, as though she didn't recognize the woman she saw there. He longed to touch her, to appear to her, to tell her that he missed her and that a moment of eternity didn't go by that he didn't think of her. But he was unable.

He watched her go to the trunk across the attic, and she unlatched it and opened the top. She pulled out a big white box that had been stored there. With slow, trembling movements, she opened it. When she pulled out her wedding dress, the one she'd worn when she'd exchanged her vows with him, he knew for sure that she was thinking of him. In spite of himself, he found comfort in that.

The dress was still white, still pure, still as beautiful as the first day she'd worn it. He watched as she slipped out of her jumper, dropped it to the floor and began stepping into the wedding dress. Confused, he sought his memory, and realized her dress for her wedding tomorrow was a pale green one that she'd bought in the designer section at Macy's. He had watched her agonize over apricot or green, church simple or formal elegant, and finally she'd chosen a pretty lace dress that Danny was going to love.

But in comparison to this dress, it was greatly lacking.

He watched, his eyes glistening as she buttoned the twenty-some-odd pearl buttons that ran from her waist to her throat, and something in his heart constricted. If only he could go back to that day, when he'd had six years with her ahead of him. If only he had those six years again....

A tear dropped from his eye as he watched her go to the mirror, standing in the dress and gazing at her reflection as if she couldn't believe the memories were that long ago. Quietly, he got up and walked behind her, and looking over her shoulder, saw her tears fall in her reflection.

She couldn't see him, couldn't know that he was there, and yet she did know somehow, he thought. She knew because he could feel that she knew. She knew because he felt their hearts were one, as they always had been. And, he suspected, as they always would be to some extent.

"Oh, Jase," she whispered with a weary sob. "I miss you."

He sucked in a breath and touched her waist, though his hand passed through it. He was no longer flesh and blood. He was spirit, and he couldn't tell her that he was here, right behind her.

She sighed and wiped her tears before they could mar the dress, and whispered, "You were right, you know. Danny does make me laugh." Instead of smiling, her face took on a tormented look. "But you know what, Jase? There's just one thing wrong. I don't think he can make me cry."

She dropped her head and hugged herself, and as he touched her with his lifeless, fleshless hands, he felt her body shaking, weeping, still grieving.

And finally he had to admit to himself that there was no peace to be gotten from watching her give herself to another man. Not for him, anyway.

"Don't worry about me," she whispered finally. "I'm going to be happy. I promised you I would."

Jason stepped around her and looked into her eyes, wishing she could see him. "You do that, Bree," he whispered. "You be happy, okay? That'll be heaven enough for me."

Unable to bear another moment of his loss, he left her there. But as he did, he couldn't tell himself any longer that everything would be all right, for now he wasn't certain that it would. She still carried too much pain. And until she was healed completely, he knew he'd never release his own.

He went to his massive mansion, with its waterfall view, and its priceless furnishings inside, and curled up on his bed to nurse his anguish for what heaven could not give him.

"THAT'S IT," Pete said, pacing the length of the conference room where Mo and Dave sat slumped over the table. "She's getting married today, and he's so miserable he can hardly get out of bed."

"Oh, he'll get out of bed to go to the wedding, all right," Mo said. "He seems to be a glutton for punishment."

"But then he'll climb back in," Dave assured them, "and there's no telling how we're ever going to get him into the mainstream of heaven."

"It's time to take the most drastic action we have," Pete said. "But before we do, I'm going upstairs for a meeting. This one is too tough for us, guys. We need help."

"I agree," Mo said. "This is a terrible responsibility. If Jason even knew we were thinking about erasing his memories, he'd probably be the first escapee we've ever had."

"It's for his own good," Dave said. "There's no other way."

"Jason Hill is going to be happy," Pete said as he started out of the room, "if it takes an act of God to make him that way."

SABRINA SLEPT LATE the day of her wedding, for she'd spent so much energy crying the night before that she needed whatever rest she could get. She spent the day packing her clothes to move over to Danny's house after the wedding, then began preparing for the ceremony.

When her mother called and asked if she could help her get ready, Sabrina told her she could be better used at the church. The simple flower arrangements would be arriving soon, and the caterer for the reception would need a few instructions.

But the truth was, she didn't want help today. She wanted to get ready alone, in the private sanctuary of her home. She wanted the reverence of quiet as she prepared for her second marriage. She wanted time to think.

She applied her makeup flawlessly, then stepped into the knee-length teal dress with the Victorian neckline that both Jason and Danny had always loved, and zipped it up in back. Quietly, she piled her hair on top of her head, not thinking about how permanent the ceremony today would be, nor how much of yesterday she would be leaving behind.

All the decisions had been made. All the plans were in order. Everything was as it was supposed to be.

When she was ready, she left her suitcase in the living room, for they had planned to come back for it after the wedding. Holding her fragile emotions as tightly as she could, she got into her car, checked her face in the rearview mirror and pulled out of the driveway.

She wondered if Jason was watching from somewhere, and if he was happy. She wondered if he felt contentment that she was finally getting what he'd wanted for her. She wondered if he could go on with his eternity now.

She drove the long way to the church, taking the rural route instead of the interstate, for she had plenty of time. As she drove beside the cotton fields and green stretches of beans almost ready for harvest, a profound sense of peace fell over her. Things were going to be fine. They were going to be good. All of heaven was with her, and God knew what was best for her.

She smiled.

As she rounded the curve ahead of her, she saw a flock of sheep clustering around a broken fence, and without warning, one tiny lamb dashed out in front of her.

Slamming on the brakes, she tried to swerve, and just at the moment that she realized she'd missed the lamb, her car went over the side of a bridge and crashed into the shallow river below.

MOMENTS LATER, the urgent sound of sirens and screeching tires descended on the previously quiet place, and paramedics ran toward the crumpled car and the witnesses who stood in despair around it.

"Get back, everybody. Let us through!" The crowd parted, and the paramedics evaluated the state of the jammed door and the condition of the woman limp behind the wheel.

It took only moments for them to remove the door and pull her out, and when they lay her on the gurney, two of the paramedics hooked her to oxygen, IVs and monitors. But the third technician held her wrist in his hand, waiting in vain for a pulse.

"We're too late," he said finally. "I think we've lost her."

JASON THOUGHT he was going to a wedding, but something had diverted him, and instead, he arrived at the scene of ambulances whining and people wailing and a crumpled car at the bank of the river.

Sabrina's car.

His heart jolted, and he saw them pull her out, lay her on the gurney and begin their frantic work to revive her. Jason burst forward.

He hurried through the crowd, though he knew no one saw him, and reached Sabrina's flaccid body on the gurney. There wasn't a mark on her, yet he knew from the looks on the paramedics' faces, and the sheet they prepared to lay over her, that they had come too late.

Could it be that the plan had been changed? Could it be that they really did understand?

Tears ambushed him, and breathing hard, afraid to hope, afraid to assume, he took her hand. She was warm, and he felt life there. Couldn't they feel that rapid pulse?

Her eyes opened, but no one seemed to see it but him. The paramedics continued their frantic work on her body as if they couldn't see that she was fine. As if they didn't know...

Jason sucked in a breath. "Baby?" he asked in panicked confusion.

Slowly, Sabrina's eyes focused on him, and she began to sit up. But as she did, her shell stayed behind, the focus of the crowd's frantic ministrations. No one saw the real Sabrina getting out of her body, sliding off the gurney and looking at Jason with astonished joy in her eyes.

And Jason realized with painful, wonderful clarity what it was he had really come here for.

Choking on a sob, she threw her arms around him, and he lifted her off the ground, holding her as tightly as he could without crushing her.

"Is this...really happening?" she asked him. "Are they going to let me come with you?"

He pressed his wet face against hers and whispered, "It looks that way, baby."

"Forever?" she asked in disbelief.

"And ever and ever and ever," he whispered. "And finally, it'll be my heaven, too."

He kissed her then, as chaos reigned around them, as sirens blared and lights flashed and people wailed, but they didn't notice any of it. They were the only two people in the world at that moment, and everything else was incidental.

Their kiss broke, and he smiled at her through his tears. "Let's go, baby," he whispered. "It's time for me to take you home."

Lifting her in his arms, he carried her through the oblivious crowd to the home he had unknowingly prepared for her.

Epilogue

Sabrina's grave was still fresh, and Danny bent down to pull a weed out of the flowers he had planted around her headstone, just like the ones he'd planted at Jason's long ago. There was a special symmetry to the graves now, he thought. Jason's had looked so lonely before, next to the huge mausoleum adjacent to it. Now he had Sabrina beside him.

Danny stood at the foot of both graves, looking from one headstone to the other, and taking out the handkerchief he'd been carrying everywhere these days, he wiped his eyes. Slowly he walked around the graves and touched Sabrina's headstone. Swerving to keep from hitting a lamb, he thought, shaking his head. There hadn't been a scratch on her. And as much as he'd grieved, and cursed, and mourned, he couldn't help believing it was all just as it should have been.

He tried to imagine her now, romping through heaven with Jason, diving headfirst into everything there. She was probably eating cookies with macadamia nuts, fishing for tarpon-size catfish, painting a masterpiece a day and cheering for Jason as he hit his home runs. Her eyes were probably lit up like two stars, and the sound of her laughter probably left the angelic choirs in awe.

Not to mention Jason.

He looked down at Jason's grave, at the place where he had helped lower the casket himself. That had been one of the two hardest days of his life. Sabrina's funeral had been the other. But even in his anguish, he had known that there was order in what had happened. There was reason. There was a plan, even if it had been amended at the very last moment.

Taking a deep breath, he touched Jason's headstone and whispered, "No hard feelings, man. Take care of her, okay?"

A sense of peace washed over him, as if he'd been bathed in some sort of cleansing tide, as if his own path had been touched by something sacred.

Still looking back, he started to walk around the mausoleum to his car waiting just beyond it, when he bumped into someone coming the other way.

The woman, a cute little thing with auburn hair and a pixie smile, almost fell. Quickly, he reached out to catch her. "I'm sorry," he said. "I didn't know anyone else was here."

She laughed. "Well, I've heard of being swept off my feet, but not *knocked* off them."

For the first time since the funeral, Danny smiled. "Are you okay?"

She arched her perfect little brows and looked at him with mischievous eyes. "I would be if someone would buy me a cup of coffee."

Danny's smile faded, and he glanced at the grave. Forcing himself to turn away, he brought his eyes to her. "All right, you're on. By the way, my name's Danny."

"Callie," she said, shaking his hand. "Nice to bump into you, and it couldn't have been in a more unlikely place, could it?"

He shook his head. "I don't know about that. I think maybe it's the *most* likely place." He touched her back and escorted her toward their cars. But just before they reached them, he stopped and frowned at her. "I'm sorry. I didn't even ask. You wouldn't happen to be here visiting the grave of a husband or boyfriend, would you?"

"Nope," she said. "My grandmother. She died last year."

His smile dawned slowly across his face. "Your grandmother," he repeated softly. "I think I can live with that."

The sound of her laughter lilting on the wind lifted his spirits instantly, and as they got into his car, he knew that everything was going to be all right.

JASON AND SABRINA lay stomach down on a downy white cloud, watching through a small window as Danny and Callie drove away. Laughing, Sabrina turned on her side and touched her husband's face. "He's going to be fine," she said.

"And so am I now," he told her. "Isn't heaven a wonderful place? Why anyone would want to be on earth is beyond me."

Her laughter played across the sky, more beautiful than a score of angels, and he rolled over and kissed her with all the passion he'd stored for three long years. And finally, he knew that eternity was just barely going to be long enough to spend with her. For theirs was a love that transcended the perfection of heaven and would stretch beyond infinity. Their heaven was in each other's joy. And their joy was in being together.

This summer, come cruising with Harlequin Books!

PORTS
OF CALL

In July, August and September, excitement, danger and, of course, romance can be found in Lynn Leslie's exciting new miniseries PORTS OF CALL. Not only can you cruise the South Pacific, the Caribbean and the Nile, your journey will also take you to Harlequin Superromance®, Harlequin Intrigue® and Harlequin American Romance®.

- ♦ In July, cruise the South Pacific with SINGAPORE FLING, a Harlequin Superromance
- ♦ NIGHT OF THE NILE from Harlequin Intrigue will heat up your August
- ♦ September is the perfect month for CRUISIN' MR. DIAMOND from Harlequin American Romance

So, cruise through the summer with LYNN LESLIE and HARLEQUIN BOOKS!

CRUISE

MILLION DOLLAR SWEEPSTAKES (III)

No purchase necessary. To enter, follow the directions published. Method of entry may vary. For eligibility, entries must be received no later than March 31, 1996. No liability is assumed for printing errors, lost, late or misdirected entries. Odds of winning are determined by the number of eligible entries distributed and received. Prizewinners will be determined no later than June 30, 1996.

Sweepstakes open to residents of the U.S. (except Puerto Rico), Canada, Europe and Taiwan who are 18 years of age or older. All applicable laws and regulations apply. Sweepstakes offer void wherever prohibited by law. Values of all prizes are in U.S. currency. This sweepstakes is presented by Torstar Corp., its subsidiaries and affiliates, in conjunction with book, merchandise and/or product offerings. For a copy of the Official Rules send a self-addressed, stamped envelope (WA residents need not affix return postage) to: MILLION DOLLAR SWEEPSTAKES (III) Rules, P.O. Box 4573, Blair, NE 68009, USA.

EXTRA BONUS PRIZE DRAWING

No purchase necessary. The Extra Bonus Prize will be awarded in a random drawing to be conducted no later than 5/30/96 from among all entries received. To qualify, entries must be received by 3/31/96 and comply with published directions. Drawing open to residents of the U.S. (except Puerto Rico), Canada, Europe and Taiwan who are 18 years of age or older. All applicable laws and regulations apply; offer void wherever prohibited by law. Odds of winning are dependent upon number of eligible entries received. Prize is valued in U.S. currency. The offer is presented by Torstar Corp., its subsidiaries and affiliates in conjunction with book, merchandise and/or product offering. For a copy of the Official Rules governing this sweepstakes, send a self-addressed, stamped envelope (WA residents need not affix return postage) to: Extra Bonus Prize Drawing Rules, P.O. Box 4590, Blair, NE 68009, USA.

SWP-H794

WEDDING SONG
Vicki Lewis Thompson

Kerry Muldoon has encountered more than her share of happy brides and grooms. She and her band—the Honeymooners—play at all the wedding receptions held in romantic Eternity, Massachusetts!

Kerry longs to walk down the aisle one day—with sexy recording executive Judd Roarke. But Kerry's dreams of singing stardom threaten to tear apart the fragile fabric of their union....

WEDDING SONG, available in August from Temptation, is the third book in Harlequin's new cross-line series, **WEDDINGS, INC.** Be sure to look for the fourth book, **THE WEDDING GAMBLE,** by Muriel Jensen (Harlequin American Romance #549), coming in September.

WED3

"GOIN' TO THE CHAPEL"

American Romance is goin' to the chapel...with three
soon-to-be-wed couples. Only thing is, saying "I do" is
the farthest thing from their minds!

Be sure you haven't missed any of the nuptials. If you have,
you can join us belatedly:

#16533	THE EIGHT SECOND WEDDING by Anne McAllister	$3.50	☐
#16537	THE KIDNAPPED BRIDE by Charlotte Maclay	$3.50	☐
#16541	VEGAS VOWS by Linda Randall Wisdom	$3.50	☐
	(limited quantities available)		

TOTAL AMOUNT	$	
POSTAGE & HANDLING	$	
($1.00 for one book, 50¢ for each additional)		
APPLICABLE TAXES*	$_____	
<u>**TOTAL PAYABLE**</u>	$_____	
(check or money order—please do not send cash)		

To order, complete this form and send it, along with a check or money order for the
total above, payable to Harlequin Books, to: **In the U.S.:** 3010 Walden Avenue,
P.O. Box 9047, Buffalo, NY 14269-9047; **In Canada:** P.O. Box 613, Fort Erie, Ontario,
L2A 5X3.

Name: _____

Address: _____ City: _____

State/Prov.: _____ Zip/Postal Code: _____

*New York residents remit applicable sales taxes.
 Canadian residents remit applicable GST and provincial taxes.

GTCF

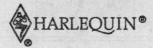

Fifty red-blooded, white-hot, true-blue hunks
from every State in the Union!

Look for MEN MADE IN AMERICA! Written by some of
our most popular authors, these stories feature fifty of the
strongest, sexiest men, each from a different state in the
union!

Two titles available every month at your favorite retail
outlet.

In July, look for:

ROCKY ROAD by Anne Stuart (Maine)
THE LOVE THING by Dixie Browning (Maryland)

In August, look for:

PROS AND CONS by Bethany Campbell (Massachusetts)
TO TAME A WOLF by Anne McAllister (Michigan)

You won't be able to resist MEN MADE IN AMERICA!

HARLEQUIN®

Don't miss these Harlequin favorites by some of our most distinguished authors!
And now you can receive a discount by ordering two or more titles!

HT #25525	THE PERFECT HUSBAND by Kristine Rolofson	$2.99	☐
HT #25554	LOVERS' SECRETS by Glenda Sanders	$2.99	☐
HP #11577	THE STONE PRINCESS by Robyn Donald	$2.99	☐
HP #11554	SECRET ADMIRER by Susan Napier	$2.99	☐
HR #03277	THE LADY AND THE TOMCAT by Bethany Campbell	$2.99	☐
HR #03283	FOREIGN AFFAIR by Eva Rutland	$2.99	☐
HS #70529	KEEPING CHRISTMAS by Marisa Carroll	$3.39	☐
HS #70578	THE LAST BUCCANEER by Lynn Erickson	$3.50	☐
HI #22256	THRICE FAMILIAR by Caroline Burnes	$2.99	☐
HI #22238	PRESUMED GUILTY by Tess Gerritsen	$2.99	☐
HAR #16496	OH, YOU BEAUTIFUL DOLL by Judith Arnold	$3.50	☐
HAR #16510	WED AGAIN by Elda Minger	$3.50	☐
HH #28719	RACHEL by Lynda Trent	$3.99	☐
HH #28795	PIECES OF SKY by Marianne Willman	$3.99	☐

Harlequin Promotional Titles

#97122	LINGERING SHADOWS by Penny Jordan	$5.99	☐
	(limited quantities available on certain titles)		

	AMOUNT	$	
DEDUCT:	10% DISCOUNT FOR 2+ BOOKS	$	
	POSTAGE & HANDLING	$	
	($1.00 for one book, 50¢ for each additional)		
	APPLICABLE TAXES*	$ _____	
	TOTAL PAYABLE	$ _____	
	(check or money order—please do not send cash)		

To order, complete this form and send it, along with a check or money order for the total above, payable to Harlequin Books, to: **In the U.S.:** 3010 Walden Avenue, P.O. Box 9047, Buffalo, NY 14269-9047; **In Canada:** P.O. Box 613, Fort Erie, Ontario, L2A 5X3.

Name: _____

Address:_____City: _____

State/Prov.: _____ Zip/Postal Code: _____

*New York residents remit applicable sales taxes.
  Canadian residents remit applicable GST and provincial taxes..

HBACK-JS